AT THE
RAINBOW'S END

AT THE RAINBOW'S END

•

SUSAN AYLWORTH

AVALON BOOKS
THOMAS BOUREGY AND COMPANY, INC.
401 LAFAYETTE STREET
NEW YORK, NEW YORK 10003

PRINTED IN THE UNITED STATES OF AMERICA
ON ACID-FREE PAPER
BY HADDON CRAFTSMEN, SCRANTON, PENNSYLVANIA

For Austin, Samantha, and Alexis, with love.
And always, for Roger.

Chapter One

A stiff breeze scoured the desert floor, catching powdery snowflakes and drifting them against the roots of the greasewood and creosote bushes. Kurt McAllister watched the would-be storm with tepid interest, idly reminded of the way his mother used to sift powdered sugar onto freshly baked gingerbread.

It had been a good meeting in Gallup that morning. If all went as planned, Rainbow Productions would soon have a contract for an exclusive series of educational videos. They had a funding proposal in for a documentary on Navajo weaving and were already paying their bills with pickup jobs for weddings, birthdays, graduations, and family reunions. In the four years since he had established his business with the woman who was now his sister-in-law, Kurt and Meg had built an inventory of successful management training programs that were bringing in steady income.

They were earning a strong reputation in the field and had recently moved into a larger storefront office in Holbrook. All was going splendidly, better than expected.

So why, Kurt wondered as he gunned the engine of his shiny new pickup and pulled into the I-40 fast lane, did he feel like chewing rails and spitting spikes? Frustration seemed to dog his heels these days, faithful as a bloodhound and not one bit prettier.

The road sign showed that Holbrook and his turnoff were still twenty-seven miles away as Kurt punched up the speed to pass a black touring car, but the added speed did nothing to decrease his restlessness. Neither did the fact that there was no apparent reason for it.

Things were going splendidly in the business. The only weak area they'd had from the beginning had been scriptwriting. Meg wrote the basic script when they did a management training video, and his brother Jim, an expert in Navajo and Hopi art, wrote most of their documentary pieces. So far, there had always been someone at the community college in Holbrook who could refine their scripts. Though he and Meg had spoken of hiring a professional scriptwriter—and they'd *have* to get someone if they got the documentary on Navajo weaving—that seemed more an opportunity than a problem. So it had to be something else that was wringing his stomach.

Whenever they had a problem in the business, Meg always sat down to analyze it. Maybe he should try . . . But thinking of Meg only made him more uneasy. Was it something about Meg that was bothering him? True, she hadn't been kicking in her usual full share in the business lately. Normally, she'd have been with him at that meeting in Gallup, but her burgeoning pregnancy was slowing her down. Kurt hadn't minded picking up the slack. Rainbow Productions was his dream, and he never would have been able to start it without his sister-in-law.

Besides, he was delighted to see Jim becoming a father. He loved Jim as he loved all the McAllister clan—fiercely, and Meg had made Jim happy. They were a dynamite couple and Kurt had no trouble imagining the beautiful, intelligent child that would result from combining those two gene pools. He fully expected to be an insufferable uncle, bragging to anyone who would listen. So the problem wasn't with Meg's contribution to the business, or with the pregnancy.

What was it then? He was thirty years old, well established in a growing business, and doing exactly what he'd always wanted to do, and still he couldn't help feeling that something important was missing from his life.

The idiot light in the small compact flashed on for the fifth time in as many miles. BRAKES, it said.

"Drat!" Alexa brought her fist down on the dash. "Now that's useful. Tell me something I don't know." She eased her foot onto the brake pedal and got mush, the same thing she'd been getting for the last twenty miles. "If I'd wanted oatmeal, I could have stopped at that greasy spoon," Alexa grumbled, pushing harder on the brake pedal and cutting back a little on her speed. She had struggled for so long, wanting what no one from Henderson had ever dared to want, and promising herself she would have it. Now here she was, touching distance from the dream of her lifetime. No way was she going to let a set of bad brakes stop her!

The last road sign had said Holbrook was only twenty-seven miles away. It was probably a risk to drive that far on spongy brakes, but she figured they'd still stop her in a crisis, and risking it was probably wiser than stopping along the shoulder of Interstate 40 in the middle of nowhere at all. She glanced at the road atlas she kept open on the passenger seat.

Holbrook didn't look like much of a town, but even if the place was positively dead, it probably had a mechanic who could work on brakes, or the master cylinder, or whatever it was that was causing that accursed idiot light to make her feel like such an idiot.

"Okay," she said aloud, determined to strike a deal with the car. "I'll coax you into Holbrook if you promise not to break down on me before we get there, okay?" She cast a worried glance at the offending light, almost expecting it to answer.

The road sign showed he was only ten miles from the turnoff when something on the road in front of him caught Kurt's eye. An ugly compact was taking a shallow curve ahead of him and not handling it well. "Take it easy," he murmured to the unseen driver. "This isn't the Daytona 500, you know." Then the compact swerved into the fast lane and back, over-correcting and nearly going off the shoulder. Kurt eased off his accelerator, sickly aware that he was about to witness an accident. "Take it—" he began again, then realized the driver wasn't the problem.

Smoke billowed from the left front wheel of the little car as the driver fought madly to keep it on the road. With a recklessness no driver would hazard, the compact swerved first to one side and then the other, screeching its tires, and finally plunged off the shoulder into the desert sand, fishtailing madly. Then the right wheels slumped into something softer, something that gave with the weight of the vehicle. Kurt watched helplessly as the car, almost in slow motion, rocked to its right, threatening to turn turtle, then righted itself, slammed into a steel fence post, and finally came to a stop.

Please protect them until I get there, Kurt prayed silently, and gunned his truck toward the crash site.

''Them'' turned out to be the driver, alone in the vehicle. She was strapped in her seat, held securely by her lap belt and shoulder harness, and apparently unconscious. The car had come to rest at something of an angle, so her upper body rested against the door and window on the driver's side of her car. Kurt thanked whatever guardian angels had been watching over her that her car door wasn't locked. It creaked when he tugged on it, but came open without much struggle. Had it not been for the harness that held her, the driver might have fallen right into Kurt's arms.

''Are you all right, miss?'' he asked aloud. He couldn't help but notice her delicate beauty. She looked to be about twenty-seven years old. The woman moaned and her eyelids fluttered in response. Kurt nodded approvingly. If she could come that close to answering, her head injury probably wasn't too bad. He gave her a quick once-over without moving her, checking for any obvious bleeding or other injuries that might require immediate attention. Finding none, except for the small bruise darkening her forehead, he left her where she was and jogged back the few yards to his truck, then used his cellular phone to call for an ambulance and tow truck. Assured they were on their way, he hurried back to his patient, who was beginning to come around. Again he was struck by how lovely she was.

"What happened?" she mumbled as he reached her.

"Beats me." Kurt gave a cursory look to the left front wheel. "It looked like maybe you had a blowout, but the tire looks okay. We'll let the mechanic decide after the tow truck gets you into town."

"Tow truck? No. Just help me get back onto the road. I have to be in Burbank tomorrow morning."

She certainly looked determined. The hard line of her jaw emphasized the valentine shape of her face. "Okay, I won't argue." Kurt kept his response amiable. "But you can't make it in this car. It's going to need some work before anyone drives it anywhere."

The driver brushed her pale hair behind one ear. A vague, confused look crossed her eyes. "Oh yeah, the brakes."

"Or something," Kurt agreed.

She made a funny face, as if she was trying for humor and couldn't quite manage it. "I guess I should beware the ides of March, huh?"

He made an effort to smile. "Listen, I didn't want to move you just in case you might have injuries I couldn't see, but if you feel like you can get out on your own . . ." He left the suggestion hanging as he opened her door.

"Yes. Okay." He could see the woman gathering her thoughts. "I just need to—" She unfastened her seat belt and tumbled into Kurt's waiting arms. "Oh!

I-I'm sorry.'' She looked up with the most beautiful sky-blue eyes he had ever seen. Kurt was instantly enthralled.

"I don't mind," he murmured, his words barely audible as a barrage of emotions battered him. "I don't mind at all." He was vaguely aware of helping the woman to her feet, but the thought that was marching through his mind like an army on the move had more to do with this lovely blond woman whom fate had just dropped into his arms, and how right it felt to hold her. He shook his head, wondering whether he might have taken a blow to the noggin too.

The woman put a hand to her head. "Oh," she said, sinking a little.

Kurt caught her under her elbow, supporting her while she steadied herself. "You hit your head pretty hard, Miss . . ." He waited, but she didn't seem to pick up on the cue. "I called an ambulance when I called the tow truck. Maybe we should—"

She moaned. "Oh no, not an ambulance. If those guys get started, I'll *never* get out of here!"

"But you're hurt—"

"Not badly. Honest. I'll be fine in no time, but I really can't afford an ambulance, or a hospital bill, or even the time it would take. I have to get back on the road again."

Kurt wavered, wondering what was the right thing to do. "Look, I'll make a deal with you. I'll cancel the ambulance if you let me give you a ride into the clinic in Holbrook. The doctor there is a friend. He can check you out quickly and I'll cover the bill myself."

"No need for that," the woman began. "Just help

me into Holbrook and I'll—'' She was reaching to close the car door as she said it, but when her left arm made contact she winced in pain.

"Whoa there!" Kurt caught her other arm, steadying her. "Let me have a look at that shoulder." He reached for her hand, but she pulled it away, cradling it against her stomach.

"No, please. Just let me—"

"I think we'd better get you to the clinic quickly," he said gently. "I'm afraid you may have broken something in there."

"Broken! No! Not now!" The news seemed to be more than she could handle. Her magnificent sky-blue eyes filled with tears. "Not when I'm so close." Her knees folded under her and Kurt helped her to the ground, then left her sitting while he went back to the truck and called again, canceling the ambulance. The flashing lights of the tow truck were approaching by the time he returned to the woman.

She was a picture of shock and pain. He'd seen it before. Growing up on a hog farm as one of four active kids, Kurt had seen his share of rough-and-tumble accidents. She was sitting, just sitting. Though tears had formed in her eyes and a stray found its way down her cheeks from time to time, she wasn't really crying. She wasn't doing anything. It was that absence of action or emotion or movement that concerned him as much as her pronounced pallor. He needed to get her to help, the quicker the better.

"The tow truck is here," he said. The monster truck was already pulling across the center divide, positioning itself to reach her car. "Let me help you to my pickup, okay?"

She nodded, looking worse than at any time since he'd first seen her. Shock was coming on fast and Kurt wondered if he'd been wise to cancel the ambulance. He slipped one arm around her waist and helped her rise. She felt warm and womanly against him as he steadied her on her feet, then walked her toward his truck. He half-lifted her into the cab of the truck and made sure she had the seat belt securely fastened, then went back to speak to the driver of the tow truck before rejoining her. It was then that he realized he didn't even know her name.

"It strikes me," he said as he joined her, "that if you're going to entrust yourself to my safekeeping, I probably ought to introduce myself. I'm Kurt McAllister. I live in Rainbow Rock, just north of Holbrook. I'm on my way home from a business meeting in Gallup, New Mexico. And you?"

"I came from Gallup too," she said.

Kurt waited, then realized that was all she planned to say. "And your name?" he prompted.

"Oh." She shook herself. "Sorry. I guess I hit my head harder than I thought. Alexa. Alexa Babbidge, from Henderson, Kentucky."

"Nice to meet you, Alexa Babbidge from Henderson, Kentucky." *Alexa*, he thought, repeating it in his mind. The name was as delicate and lovely as the woman herself. "And what brings you through our neck of the woods?"

The panic reentered Alexa's lovely eyes. "I have an appointment, a very important appointment, in Burbank tomorrow morning. Really, if there's any way we can get me back on the road, any way at all . . ." She paused, apparently out of steam.

Kurt decided maybe it would be wise to get her to talk about it. "So what is it that's so important in Burbank?"

"It's sort of like . . . like a job interview."

"If it's an interview, they'll understand why you're late, and reschedule," he said, trying to make his explanation sound as sensible to her as it did to him.

"I'm afraid it isn't that simple."

Kurt noticed she was looking paler. He hoped he could get her to the clinic in Holbrook before she passed out cold in his cab.

As it was, she was leaning against the door of his truck, holding her left arm tight against her chest, by the time he pulled up at the clinic. He opened her door and offered his arm, then saw how fragile she looked and decided to hurry things along. "Hang on, Alexa," he said as he unbuckled her seat belt and slid one arm under her knees. "We're going for a little ride."

"I can walk. Really," she protested, but didn't seem to have the energy to pursue the idea as Kurt cradled her against him.

"This is easier," he murmured, adding to himself that it was also a lot more fun. She was all woman in his arms—strong, firmly muscled, with just the right degree of feminine softness. He'd been intrigued by her from the moment he'd first seen her face. When she sighed and put her arm around his neck, snuggling against his chest, he felt a rush of tenderness that threatened to overwhelm him.

He pushed through the front door and past the three people in the waiting room. "Excuse me, Myra," he said to the woman behind the front desk. "I have an emergency here. I'm taking her right through to the examining room.''

The woman, caught in the midst of raising her hand in protest, used it to smooth her graying hair instead. "That will be fine, Kurt," she said. "Use room three, please.''

"Room three it is." Kurt pushed into the main hall-way, located room three, and tenderly placed his patient on the table. "I've got a bit of a quandary here," he said, talking calmly as he gathered the available pillows and stacked them on the examining table. "You probably need to get your head down, but your shoulder will likely throb like the devil if you do. I think the best option might be to have you recline on these pillows. There, lie back straight. Like that," he said, straightening the pillows behind her. "Think you can manage on your own for a minute? I'd like to try to find you some ice for that lump on your head."

She nodded, smiling weakly.

"I'll be right back." Kurt slipped out of the room, then strode down the hallway, his boots beating out a rapid tattoo as he found the doctor's supplies and helped himself to an ice bag, filling it at the machine in the corner.

"Well, Kurt, I see you're making yourself at home." Dr. Kemp adjusted the stethoscope around his neck and offered Kurt his hand as he shut the door to room one behind him. "Which McAllister am I seeing today?''

"This one's a special case, doc," Kurt answered. "She lost control of her car about eight miles out on I-40. I figure her left shoulder's hurt, possibly broken, but she hit her head too. She was unconscious when

I got to her and she's looking pale and shocky, maybe a mild concussion.''

The doctor, who had learned to trust Kurt's untrained but experienced diagnoses, told Myra to tell the patient in room two that he'd be delayed, and followed Kurt down the hall.

Half an hour later, Kurt's diagnosis was confirmed—all except the shoulder, which turned out to be sprained, but not broken. Alexa found herself being helped into a wheelchair, her arm in a sling. "But I can't stay," she argued weakly, fighting back tears. "You don't understand. I have to be in Burbank tomorrow morning. I *have* to!"

"Not in *your* car," Kurt said. "I just checked with the garage. It looks like you blew a wheel bearing. It'll take a couple of days to get the parts for that, and there was damage to the undercarriage when you went off the road."

"Then I'll rent a car," Alexa said, determined not to let anything keep her from her dreams.

"Not tonight. You simply cannot drive tonight, young lady," the doctor said, his tone even more patronizing than his words. "You are in no condition. You're suffering a mild concussion and some degree of shock. Add that up and you are legally impaired. If you attempted to drive, I'd be obligated to stop you."

Alexa heard the words and let them register, still unwilling to accept that her dreams could end like this. "There has to be a way," she said, searching the men's faces, then appealing to the handsome cowboy who had been such a gentle rescuer. "How about a bus? Surely there's a bus line that comes through on I-40.''

''Sure there is,'' the cowboy answered. She struggled to remember his name. Karl? Kirk, maybe? ''The westbound stops through twice a day down at the depot.'' He looked at his watch, then shook his head. ''I'm afraid the afternoon bus has already gone. It'll be early tomorrow before there's another one headed that way.''

''That's too late.'' She pursed her lips. ''A plane?'' she asked hopefully. If she added up everything in her purse, she might have enough for a ticket.

The doctor answered. ''Not going *that* way. Not unless you charter. The only regular route is between here and Phoenix, and I don't think they fly again until tomorrow.''

Alexa sighed, letting reality sink in. A single tear slid down her cheek. ''I'm going to miss it,'' she said quietly. ''All this time, all this way, and now I'm going to miss it.''

The cowboy laid his hand over hers. ''I'm sure you can reschedule. Come on. Let's find a phone.''

Alexa didn't feel the same certainty, but she nodded anyway. ''Thanks, doctor,'' she said, remembering her manners as she left. Until then, it hadn't occurred to her to wonder how her costs were being covered. She turned to the cowboy. ''Where do I pay?''

''Don't worry about it,'' he said. ''It's covered.''

She drew together what little energy she still felt. ''I can't allow that,'' she said. ''I don't have a lot, but I can pay my own bills.''

The cowboy waved her away. ''It's nothing,'' he said. ''We have a long-standing account here, both for the family and the farm workers. Dr. Kemp will just add it to the bill.''

"Really, I must insist . . ." She wished she could remember his name.

"Good-bye, Kurt," the gray-haired receptionist said as he wheeled Alexa past the front desk. The cowboy nodded in response.

"I really must insist, Kurt," Alexa continued, grateful for the timely intervention. "I like to pay my own way."

"Tell you what," the cowboy, Kurt, said. Alexa could tell he was going to adopt that reasonable tone again. "Let's go with it the way it is for now. Myra will put it on the family account and everything will be fine. Then when things work out for you and you get that great job you're going after in Burbank, you can send a check."

Alexa opened her mouth to protest, then remembered how little she had in her purse. Her adventure had been a comedy of errors since she'd left Kentucky; *everything* had cost more than expected. Maybe she should just be grateful for this Samaritan—a rather nice-looking Samaritan—and let things stand as they were. "All right," she acquiesced. "Thank you."

"No problem," he said, then helped her out of the wheelchair and into the truck. "Give me a minute to get this contraption back inside, then we'll find you a phone."

"I'll need one that takes coins," Alexa said as he returned, wishing she'd gotten around to applying for a phone card. She was already formulating her speech for the man in Burbank, hoping against every expectation that it would be convincing enough.

*   *   *

Kurt watched nervously as Alexa leaned against the door of the phone booth. Based on her expression and body language, the conversation wasn't going well. He wondered what kind of job interview would bring someone all the way from Kentucky to— Then it struck him. Burbank. She was headed for Burbank. Some of the biggest studios in Hollywood weren't really in Hollywood at all.

An aspiring actress? She certainly had the looks. He guessed she was about five-eight, and he knew from holding her that she was fashionably thin and very fit, though she certainly had her share of feminine curves. She had a face all her own—unquestionably beautiful, but not that cookie-cutter Barbie-doll look that seemed to be on all the magazine covers. No, there was something delicate and winsome and utterly charming about her features. Combine that with the soft frame of silver-blond hair that fell about her face in a gentle pageboy cut and those startling, sky-blue eyes, and Hollywood would be hard-pressed to find an ingenue any lovelier.

Her voice was also a plus. He remembered it, savoring the few times she had spoken. It was warm and melodic, rich and full, the kind of voice that made a man think of gentle evenings curled up in front of a fireplace. No doubt about it—Alexa had the voice to be the next Hollywood discovery. The realization made him feel proud of her, proud to know her, more than a little possessive, and certain he didn't want her to go.

As she hung up the phone, the look on her face

spoke volumes. She quickly made another call, then joined him in the truck.

"Couldn't reschedule?" he asked, hoping he didn't sound too pleased.

"Oh, he let me reschedule, all right—for the first of May."

"May? But that's—"

"More than five weeks," Alexa finished for him. "His series has been picked up as a summer replacement and they're going into production on some new episodes the day after tomorrow. If I could have made it tomorrow, I might have been working by Thursday afternoon. As it is, he'd rather not talk to me until the first of May." She shrugged.

Kurt could see her eyes filling with unshed tears. "So what now?" he asked.

Alexa shrugged. "I don't know. I called my family to let them know about the change in plans. I guess the first thing is to find some place to stay for a few days until my car is roadworthy, then I'll head for California and get work someplace until I can keep my appointment."

"I'm sure you'll have no trouble," Kurt told her, thinking that he'd hire her in a snap if he were making a movie or a TV series. But wait a minute! He *was* making movies, wasn't he? "Listen, maybe we can work something out. My mom has a couple of spare rooms at the farm, now that my brother Jim and I have both moved out on our own. I'm sure she wouldn't mind having you there for a few days—"

"Out of the question." Alexa cut him off. "It's one thing to let you cover my doctor bills, even on loan.

It's something else entirely to move in on your family.''

"It would be no problem," Kurt assured her, delighted to have found the perfect solution.

"I can't pay you what room and board is worth," Alexa answered. "Please. Just find me a simple hotel room. I'll take it from there."

"Payment is no problem." The cowboy was giving her an eager look—too eager, Alexa thought suddenly. "I'm sure we can think of something . . ."

For the first time since he had come to her rescue, Alexa was wary of the man in the cab. She toughened her voice. "Look, cowboy. I don't know if you're suggesting what it sounds like, but—"

The cowboy blushed. He actually *blushed*. "Oh no, ma'am," he said. "Sorry to give you the wrong impression. What I mean is, I own a business and we could use some help around the place—simple things, like answering phones and such. Since you're going to be looking for a job anyway, why don't you just stick around here until it's time to head for Burbank? Mom will enjoy your company out at the farm and I can use your help around the shop. What do you think?''

"What kind of shop?" Alexa asked, still wary.

"Rainbow Productions. My sister-in-law and I make instructional videotapes and documentaries."

Alexa smiled. To Kurt, it looked like dawn rising over the desert. "Really? You make movies out of Holbrook, Arizona?"

"Well, yeah." Kurt decided to play his trump card. "You're in movies too, aren't you?" She nodded. "You're an actress?"

Alexa felt her breath catch in her throat, then let it out in a surprised giggle. "Me? Acting? I'm scared to death of cameras!"

"Then . . ." The unspoken question sat between his eyebrows.

"I'm a writer," she said, tipping up her chin. "With a little luck, by mid-June I'll be a screenwriter."

Kurt blessed the Fates as he smiled back at her. "Alexa," he announced, "we do have something to talk about."

Chapter Two

Alexa sat behind her desk at Rainbow Productions. She was supposed to be studying the script for an upcoming video entitled *"Team Management of Projects."* What she was covertly studying was the owner of the company.

Even a woman with blinders on—and Alexa had been wearing blinders since she had first stated her ambition to be a screenwriter—couldn't help but notice that her cowboy Samaritan was a hunk. She estimated his height at about six-two, tall enough to make her feel tiny. Add that to shoulder-length golden hair, a splendid tan, and a physique to die for, and it made for one fine-looking man. Even with a dog's face, he'd have turned heads, but Kurt McAllister had a face made for movie close-ups. His forehead was broad, his hazel-green eyes well spaced, his nose long and straight. His brows were thick but tidy, his cheekbones high and strong, his jaw square. His was an altogether beautiful masculine face. Only the lips suggested a more delicate look. The rest of his face was rugged, manly. The lips were a giveaway that there was a sensual, sensitive soul inside—the lips and the dimples, Alexa corrected as Kurt looked up, caught her watching him, and sent her another dazzling smile.

Life wasn't fair; Alexa knew that. Still, it took some kind of Machiavellian maneuvering to have her meet Mr. Could-be Right just on the verge of realizing her dreams—hundreds of miles away.

"How's it coming, Alexa?"

"Hmm?" Caught daydreaming, Alexa tried to approximate a businesslike look before she turned her eyes to meet Kurt's.

"I asked how it's coming," he repeated amiably.

Oh, my! Alexa exclaimed to herself. If looks weren't enough, a voice as smooth as Kurt's was probably illegal in at least fifteen states. She tried to remember the notes she'd made that morning, but had to stare at the printed page to get her mind back on her work. "Not bad, actually. Meg has a nice hand with a script. The jargon gets a little heavy in spots, though, and that sometimes makes for wordiness. Like the title, for instance."

Kurt raised an eyebrow. "You have a problem with the title?"

"Not really, but why 'Team Management of Projects'? Why not 'Team Project Management'? It's only one word shorter, but it gets the preposition out of there and leaves the emphasis on the word 'management,' which is, after all, the skill you're selling."

Kurt looked at the script, idly rubbing his chin.

"You're right," he concluded. "I wouldn't have noticed. It seems like a small thing, but it makes a big difference." He handed it back to her. "You're good at this."

"I try." She turned her attention back to the script, thinking she'd darn well better be good. She'd been doing this for years now, wherever she could get work in anything close to the business, trying to prove herself and build a portfolio—all in the hope that someday she could wangle an interview with a major studio. Now, only a day away and . . . She frowned at the sling that encased her left arm.

But why rehash it? What was done was done, and— she hazarded a look at Kurt's broad shoulders as he walked away—there *were* compensations.

Even staying at the pig farm was fun. Kate McAllister, Kurt's mom, had turned out to be an utterly charming hostess, reminding Alexa of her own mother—minus several children and seventy or eighty pounds. Alexa would probably gain those pounds herself if Kate kept cooking the way she had for the past three days. Alexa couldn't remember ever having stuffed pork chops, homemade applesauce, and fresh cherry cobbler all in the same meal.

Then there was Chris. The youngest McAllister brother still lived at the farm. Two years her senior and every bit as good-looking as the older blond prototype, Chris was cute, flirty, and easy to be around— a real relief, Alexa admitted, from the intensity she felt whenever she was near his older brother. While Chris offered simple, uncomplicated fun, Kurt's intense gaze spoke of children and white picket fences and growing old together before the backdrop of ten thousand western sunsets. Okay, so maybe it was her imagination—or even wishful thinking—but she'd swear that when Kurt looked at her, he had forever in mind.

Meg had noticed it too. Kurt's sister-in-law and business partner had come out to the house to meet Alexa on Wednesday, the day Kurt had insisted Alexa save for rest and recuperation, then she'd been in early yesterday to help Alexa adjust to her first day in the office.

Alexa had taken an immediate liking to Meg, despite the fact that the hugely pregnant woman's condition made her nervous. They'd started with small talk about Alexa's accident and Meg's pregnancy, but it hadn't taken Meg long to cut through to meatier matters. "Kurt tells me you may soon be indispensable to this business."

"Did he also tell you I have a chance-of-a-lifetime interview in Burbank on the first of May?"

"Yes, and he told me he plans to make Rainbow Productions so attractive that you'll choose to stay here instead."

Alexa hesitated, doubting whether it was the business that Kurt wanted her to be attracted to. "No offense, Meg, but there are all kinds of independent studios where I could be working if that's what I wanted. There's only one So Fein Productions."

Meg looked impressed. "So Fein as in Joshua Fein? The producer of half the top-rated shows on television?"

"The same. My appointment is with the head writer. If all goes as I hope, I'll soon be on the writing staff for a new period drama they're putting on as a summer replacement. It may be one of the hottest things going in the new fall season.''

"I know it—it's called 'Mountain Magic.' " Meg giggled, then mimicked the television promo. "The story of a young city woman recruited to teach school in the hill country of Appalachia."

"That's the one," Alexa answered.

"Wow. And you have a chance to be on the writing team. I'm impressed."

Alexa shrugged. "So am I. I've dreamed of writing for television ever since I was in high school, but I never believed I might get a chance to start at the top. You can see why it's so important to me."

Meg nodded. "Yes, I can. Kurt's going to be terribly disappointed when you leave us, though."

Alexa chose to believe they were talking business. "Good scriptwriters aren't that hard to find. Besides, you've got plenty of talent at the business yourself, and what you don't know now, you'll learn as you practice."

"It's not just the business and you know it. I've seen the way Kurt looks at you. You can't have failed to notice."

"I've noticed." Alexa pursed her lips. "What I want to know is, why me? The man couldn't possibly lack for female companionship, not with a build like that!"

Meg's look was smugly possessive. "He *is* good-looking, isn't he?"

"Spectacular," Alexa agreed.

"And strong," Meg added.

Alexa nodded. "He looks like he could bench press a small city." Then she breathed out a deep sigh. "So why is he interested in a highway castoff who's just passing through?''

''Don't cut yourself short, Alexa. You're beautiful, intelligent, witty, a talented writer . . . Kurt knows a good thing when he sees it.''

''But I'm—''

''On your way to Burbank. I know. I heard.''

But the conversation with Meg was only the first salvo in what quickly took shape as a well-orchestrated battle plan. ''You know, Alexa,'' Kurt told her as they closed the shop together that Friday evening, ''what you're doing with that management training script is nothing short of amazing. You're a very talented writer.''

''Well, thank you, Kurt.'' Alexa, left arm in a sling, shouldered her purse with her right. ''I like to think I know what I'm doing.''

''It's more than that.'' Kurt locked the door securely. ''You have the kind of skill that makes the difference between good enough and great.''

''Thank you again.'' Alexa nodded acknowledgment, more than a little uneasy with all this praise.

''You know, you're exactly what we need around here—on a permanent basis, I mean. If you ever decide you want a home at Rainbow Productions, I'll do my best to pay you whatever it takes.''

Alexa slowly lifted one eyebrow. ''You're offering me a job?''

''A permanent position as head writer. All you have to do is say so, and it's yours.''

''Isn't this a little quick? I've only been here a couple of days.''

''I know what I've seen you do in those couple of

days. You're good, Alexa, and you work well with both Meg and me. We can use you." He took both her elbows, being careful of her sore shoulder, and turned her toward him so she couldn't fail to see his eyes. "We'd love to have you stay."

"Kurt, you know this is temporary for me. It has to be. I have an opportunity waiting for me in California that's just too good to pass up."

Kurt let his hands drop to his sides. "I thought you'd say that," he said, "but the offer's open, any time you want it."

"Thank you. I'm very flattered."

Flattered didn't begin to describe what she was feeling, Alexa reflected that evening as she dressed for bed in the warm, cozy room that had once been Kurt's. No indeed, life was *not* fair.

Life wasn't fair, Kurt reflected as he drove away from his mother's home that Friday evening. Life had found the one perfect woman in all the world and literally dropped her into his arms. Only she didn't agree that she was the perfect woman and insisted she was just passing through, giving him only five weeks to persuade her she was wrong.

Worse yet, when he'd cooked up the idea of having her stay with his mother, he hadn't counted on Chris as part of the equation. According to his plan, he would be able to show up every evening after work, tenderly wooing and courting Alexa before she even realized what he was doing. As it was, when he'd stopped in to visit the night before, he'd found her curled up on the couch in his mother's parlor, her knees beneath her and one of his mom's patchwork quilts wrapped around her, as brother Chris showed her the family album. It had been quite a picture— Alexa and Chris cozied up on the sofa, chuckling at family photos and getting more than one good belly laugh at his expense. Well, if Chris thought he was going to roll over and play dead, he had another think coming!

Kurt noticed his speedometer climbing toward seventy miles per hour and, shamefaced, backed off the accelerator. He should have learned years ago that speed was no antidote for stupidity. No matter how quickly he drove to or from Alexa, the obstacles would still be there.

"Aw, heck. Who do I think I'm kidding?" he asked aloud. Alexa wasn't planning to stay. She'd made that plenty clear from the beginning. "So why don't I just shut up and let her drive away?" He directed the question into the vast beyond, hoping that whatever higher power had orchestrated this little drama would let him exit before the final act. Even as he asked it, he already knew the answer.

Maybe he wasn't in love with Alexa. He probably hadn't known her long enough for love to be part of the scene. But he liked her. He liked her an awful lot, and he wasn't going to let her go without giving it one heckuva try.

"Yeah, that sounds great," Kurt said for probably the fourteenth time in a row, responding to Alexa's narrative. He'd spent yesterday away from her to handle some personal business and, when he stopped to think about it, to give himself some perspective. Maybe it was nothing more than coincidence that had made him feel so instantly drawn to her. Maybe she wasn't really as beautiful, as perfect, as he remembered.

Now here he sat in the old family dining room, supposedly enjoying Sunday dinner with the clan, and finding himself more drawn to Alexa today than ever. In her blue jeans and sandals and a soft blue sweater that emphasized the color of her eyes, she was a picture to make any man's heart race. Worse yet, it was obvious that staying away Saturday had been a mistake. Chris, who now sat on the other side of Alexa, had clearly been busy. Since Kurt had arrived this morning, he'd heard about their tour of the pig farm; their ride into Holbrook to buy feed together; their walk out through the cornfield; their slow, easy drive to the river in the dune buggy and their impromptu decision to go wading.

Alexa had smiled and laughed frequently throughout the recitation. She and Chris looked like a couple, already sharing private jokes and glances. Chris couldn't seem to keep his hands to himself, Kurt noted sourly. He was constantly touching Alexa's hand or sliding his arm across the back of her chair. If he patted her knee one more time, Kurt wasn't sure he could be responsible for his actions.

Just then Chris laughed and patted Alexa's knee. Kurt was halfway out of his chair before he remembered he was sitting in his mother's house with women and children present. When Chris looked up and asked, "Something the matter, bro?" Kurt had to fight down the urge to bare his teeth and growl.

So what's my situation here? he asked himself as he resumed his seat, assuring everyone he was fine.

He had to admit it didn't look good. He was madly attracted to a woman who didn't want to be here and who frankly seemed to prefer his younger brother. He'd already told her he wanted her to stay, and had been politely but thoroughly rejected. Now he sat at the family dinner table, aching to pull her into his arms, and watching her flirt with his little brother instead.

Kurt took a deep breath, hoping to steady his queasy stomach. Life wasn't fair at all.

" 'I'll take you home again, Kathleen,' " the family sang, and Alexa joined in happily. The Sunday family dinner at the McAllister home was much like Sunday dinners she remembered from her childhood in Henderson, but the after-dinner sing-along was a distinct, added plus. The many discordant Babbidges had never harmonized as this group did.

Alexa was enjoying them all. Until today, she hadn't had a chance to meet Meg's husband, Jim, the eldest of the McAllister brothers. He was taller even than Kurt and just as spectacularly handsome. He was also a tender husband, hovering over Meg so attentively that Meg finally had to tell him to go find something to do before he drove her crazy. Alexa had chatted with him earlier when the family was clearing the table and had found Jim fascinating to talk to, full of interesting facts about Native American art and stories gathered from intimate observations of Navajo life. He was eager for the coming birth too, and kept pointing out that he'd be a father in less than two months. Alexa had responded that he was a father already, and Jim had moaned and gone slightly pale.

The other family members new to Alexa were Joan, eldest in the family, her husband Bob, and their three children: Alice, who was almost eight, Tyler, who was six, and little Cassie who would soon be two. They were a handful, but Joan managed them well. The children were well behaved and respectful. Alexa found them all delightful.

The one McAllister who was giving her fits was the one who had brought her here. When it came to Kurt, Alexa was clueless.

Since the minute she'd opened her eyes and fallen into his arms, he had treated her like a long-lost love. He'd been nothing less than a godsend in those first hours, not only getting her through the accident, but finding medical aid and arranging a place for her to stay, even providing her with enjoyable, meaningful work. He had taken her into his family and treated her like she was made of crystal. Then he'd vanished.

She hadn't seen him Friday evening or all day Saturday. Today he'd shown up for the family dinner and had sat right next to her at the table, but he'd still been as distant as Mt. Everest—and almost as cold.

"Was it something I said?" she asked Meg when Kurt watched her pick up the verse on "Goodnight, Sweetheart" and immediately left the room.

"Hard to guess," Meg answered, "but I wouldn't be surprised if it has something to do with the way Chris is moving in on you."

Alexa wrinkled her nose. "You know I'm not serious about Chris."

"You're not serious about Kurt, either."

Alexa nodded. "True."

Meg's look was knowing. "I think there's your problem in a nutshell."

Alexa pondered that as the family gathered for leftovers and apple pie, but she made a point of keeping some distance between herself and Chris, hoping it might ease Kurt's mind. It was the least she could do for someone who had been so . . . kind.

Kurt stood on the front porch of his family home, listening to Alexa's honeyed alto. It was torture, sweet torture. If he thought he could get away with it, he'd leave in a country minute.

"What's up, partner?"

Kurt looked up, startled to see Meg approach. "I didn't know you were out here."

"Obviously." Meg nodded toward the window where they could both see Alexa singing. "The lady is really getting to you, isn't she?"

Kurt practically growled. "Mind your own business, sis."

Meg grinned. "I *am* minding my business," she said, ever so sensibly. "Alexa is working in my business, remember? Whatever is eating you, I'd like to see you work it out before you come to the office tomorrow. We could be hearing about the funding for the documentary any day now, and if we get it, I'm going to need you on your toes—and able to work with the help."

"I'm the one who hired her," he said with a snarl.

Still untroubled by Kurt's surly mood, Meg smiled again. "Looks like it's going to be a lovely sunset. The new snow from last night will reflect all the colors. Should be a great view of it from the hills south of town.''

Kurt scowled, refusing to take the bait.

''I'd take the truck if I were you. You know, bench seat and all?''

Kurt gave her a look designed to chill her to her toes. ''Why don't you tell Chris about it?''

''I could, I suppose, but I'm telling you.''

That finally elicited a wry grin. ''You're quite a partner, you know that?''

''Absolutely,'' Meg agreed, tossing her hair as she went back into the house. Kurt smiled as he watched her go.

''You're right. It's spectacular,'' Alexa said as she watched the brilliant sunset glitter off the fresh blanket of snow. ''Thanks for inviting me.''

''Thanks for coming.'' Kurt released his seat belt and slid closer, putting his arm around her, but careful not to crowd her injured shoulder. ''I wanted to talk to you anyway—outside the office, I mean.''

Alexa stiffened. This wasn't going to be another attempt to change her mind about Burbank, was it?

''I wanted to apologize if it seemed like I was putting pressure on you,'' Kurt said, repeating the lines he'd been rehearsing to himself, hoping they sounded genuine. ''I realize you're looking at the chance of a lifetime out in California and well, I just want you to know I wish you all the best.'' He turned to look into her gorgeous eyes, convinced he could make this sound real. ''I really hope you get that job. You deserve it, Alexa.''

Alexa sighed in relief. "Thank you, Kurt. I appreciate that."

"I just didn't want to make you uncomfortable," Kurt said, knowing this was the right thing to do, and wishing he could tell her how he really felt—that is, assuming he could figure it out.

"I guess I have been a little uneasy," she agreed.

Kurt noticed that she rested against him as she relaxed. He decided not to mention that she hadn't seemed the least bit uneasy with his little brother. "I'm sorry about that. My only intention was to let you know what a superior job I think you're doing for us."

"Thanks." Alexa relaxed against him. "Just look at that beautiful sky!"

Things were easier between them then, and they enjoyed both the sunset and each other's company as they chatted about the roots of Kurt's business and what Alexa would like to do with "Mountain Magic." Kurt was careful not to crowd Alexa in any way and she rewarded him by staying near and touching him often. Even more important to Kurt, she didn't mention Chris for the rest of the evening. If watching her with Chris this afternoon had been torture, then surely this evening was heaven—heaven and a little bit more. By the time he drove her back to the farm some three hours later, he was fairly certain they could work together comfortably.

He walked her to the porch, then held the front door for her. "Good night, Alexa," he said, determined to be the perfect gentleman. "Thanks for coming out with me this evening."

"Thanks for inviting me," she answered, then stood on tiptoe and brushed her lips lightly against his.

Kurt hadn't expected the kiss, but he responded as if he'd been waiting for it all his life. What began as a light brush lingered and warmed as Alexa went boneless in his arms and his whole soul yearned toward her. Long seconds later, he released her, awestruck by what they had just shared.

"See you, uh, tomorrow," Alexa said as she drew away. He thought she looked as stunned as he felt. The last thing he saw as the door closed behind her was her startling eyes, sparkling like silver dollars and almost as large.

Kurt stood on the porch, his heart ready to leap right out of his chest and tap-dance on the deck. "Yeah, tomorrow," he mumbled, but she was gone for a full two minutes before he could walk down the steps to his truck. He drove home slowly, savoring the moment.

It had been a test, an experiment, Alexa assured herself as she lay in Kurt's old bed, unable to sleep. Chris had kissed her when they were at the river Saturday—just a quick kiss, a surprise she hadn't seen coming. It was pleasant enough as kisses went, maybe a four on her one-to-ten kisses scale, but it hadn't had any effect on her breathing or heart rate. It hadn't made her wish for cozy picnic blankets or long afternoons in the shade. Kissing Kurt had been a comparison test, like the ones in the supermarket where you tried Brand X and the company brand, then told the tester which you liked better and why.

Only there was no tester to record the results of this

experiment, and no one at all to rescue Alexa from its consequences. Had she ever felt this kind of intense, soul-searing heat? Certainly no simple touch of the lips had ever made her want what she wanted now, or think what she was now thinking. Chris's kiss had been a momentary diversion; Kurt's was a taste of eternity, and it promised such passion and depth and intensity that she shuddered with the power of it. If a touch as brief and light as that could make her feel like this, she was going to have to invent a new kisses scale!

"Oh, Kurt, what are you doing to my good intentions?" she moaned at the ceiling. The only way she'd be able to face him tomorrow was if she kept things on a strictly business basis and never, *ever* allowed another test kiss.

"Great news, everybody!" Meg burst through the door at Rainbow Productions, waving an envelope in the air. "We've got the funding. The documentary on Navajo weaving is a go!"

"That's wonderful, Meg!" Careful of the baby, Kurt grabbed his partner from the side and whirled her around fully once before setting her feet back on the floor. "This is going to be the best piece we've ever done."

"Our masterpiece," Meg agreed. "Our magnum opus!"

Alexa watched from a distance, happy for them and sharply aware that she had no part in their celebration. By the time they'd finished their magnum opus, she would be long gone and settled somewhere else, maybe producing a magnum opus of her own. She was picturing herself humbly accepting an Emmy for her work on "Mountain Magic" when Meg grabbed her by the hand.

"Come on, Alexa, you've got to get in on this too."

"But I'm not going to be here. I'm on my way to that interview in—"

"Burbank." Kurt and Meg spoke simultaneously, and the laughter that followed broke the tension Alexa had felt all morning.

"You'll be here for another month," Kurt said, picking up on her cue, "and we can really use your help during that time. With a little luck, we can have most of the script roughed out before you go."

Alexa nodded. "That sounds reasonable."

"See?" Meg was beaming. "You do get a piece of this action."

Meg ordered a pizza for Kurt and Alexa and a bland sandwich for herself and they all worked through lunch, sketching out a plan for how to get much of the preproduction done in the coming four weeks. Jim came in at mid-afternoon and went over it with them, analyzing where they might need more research and advising them on which weavers would likely be the most helpful in getting the information and visuals they needed. By closing time, they had a plan for where they'd be each day for the coming month. Alexa couldn't help noticing that it involved a lot of travel with Kurt. Luckily for her sanity, Meg was going along.

"I don't know about this last week," Jim was saying as Alexa tuned in again. He was looking critically at their schedule. "It's probably not wise for Meg to be that far away that close to due date."

"I can travel then. I'll still be more than three weeks away," Meg complained, but Jim was adamant.

"Don't argue, love. For my own peace of mind it's important that I know you're not delivering on some washboard road outside of Tuba City. Humor me."

Meg nuzzled her husband's cheek. "Anything for you, you gorgeous hunk." She patted his back pocket and got an embarrassed "Hey!" for her efforts.

"Cut it out, you two," Kurt teased. "There are ladies present." But it was obvious to everyone that Kurt and Alexa were both enjoying the couple's playful affection.

By the time she and Kurt closed the shop that evening, Alexa was feeling more at ease, and more a part of things, than she had at any time since arriving in Rainbow Rock. "I've been thinking about one problem we didn't work out today," she said as Kurt started the truck.

Kurt raised an eyebrow. "I thought we were fairly thorough."

"It isn't about the project, specifically. It's more about how the office will run without us when you and Meg and I are doing research on the reservation."

"Good point," Kurt conceded. "And one I hadn't thought of."

"Remember when you first talked to me about working here?" Alexa went on. "You talked about answering phones and such, and I've been doing that, along with looking at your scripts. The orders have been steady, and even though you have those high school kids coming in to fill them every day after school, someone is going to have to be in the office during the day."

"The order line and answering machine have worked fine until now . . ." Kurt began, then realized that either he or Meg had been in the office most of the time for the past several months. "But you're right. I guess we'll have to look for somebody." Kurt turned the truck up the drive to the farm.

"We've still got a few days before we start the out-of-town work," Alexa added helpfully. "If you want to run an ad or something, I'll be able to help interview and train someone."

"That sounds good. I'll look into it first thing in the morning." Kurt stopped the truck and walked Alexa toward the door, a look of anticipation on his face.

Alexa knew what he was expecting; it was practically written on his forehead. Well, no time like the present to test her new resolve. "Thanks for the ride," she said, and slipped through the door before anything could happen. "I'll see you in the morning, okay?"

"Yeah, sure." Kurt's disappointment barely showed. "See you in the morning."

"Good night," Alexa said, and closed the door behind her, only half certain that her close escape had been a good idea. She sighed. No one had ever told her life was fair.

Chapter Three

Alexa slipped her quarters into the slots and pushed the coin holder into the machine. The washer started instantly, temporarily restoring her faith in major appliances. She'd frequently feared they were out to harm her.

She started a second machine for her whites—this one, surprisingly, worked as well as the first—and settled down with the new novel she'd picked up in town. It was dark outside and the March wind howled like an animal in agony, carrying light flurries of snow. Alexa shuddered. Maybe she should have taken Kate up on her offer to do her laundry at the farm. Her excuse was a desire to get some fresh air; her reality was a need for distance, a little space between herself and the wonderful, confusing McAllister clan.

She was just getting into her novel when a woman entered the Laundromat, towing a heavy clothes bag.

38

Alexa probably wouldn't have noticed except for the two children who dragged in behind.

"Did not!" the boy, about seven, declared as he came through the door.

"Did so!" His sister, probably about ten, was right behind him, grabbing at his hair.

"Lydia! Danny! Stop that *now*!" the woman ordered.

She looked tired, Alexa thought as she watched the woman set down the heavy bag, then put the boy and girl in separate chairs on either side of the magazine table.

"Here's your coloring book, Danny. Remember? You wanted to do at least two pages tonight. Lydia, where's that book you were reading?"

"Danny made me leave it in the car." The girl pouted.

"Did not," Danny answered on cue.

"Did—"

"Danny didn't make you do anything," the mother said patiently. "Now go to the car and get it. You can read while I start the wash."

The girl got up, grumbling under her breath about the inequities involved in having little brothers, and the woman started loading laundry into four machines, separating colors and fabrics as she went. There was no question that they were a family. The children had the same near-black hair, dark eyes, and olive skin as their mother, and the same lovely features.

The girl returned with her book and settled down to read; her mother soon sat next to her with a magazine. Things were quiet for a time until the girl gave an exaggerated sigh and thumped her book down.

"Something wrong?" the woman asked.

"It's boring," the girl complained. "You seem to think I'm a child, Mother. I don't know why you always get me such boring books." She rolled her eyes in a gesture that suggested mothers must be the stupidest souls on earth. Alexa covered an amused smile, burying her nose in her book.

"You can read a magazine if you like," the mother answered. Alexa could tell her patience was strained, but she was maintaining a thoroughly admirable tone with the child. "They're written for grown-ups."

"They're all so . . . ." The girl paused for emphasis. "So pe-des-tri-an."

The mother looked suitably impressed. "Pedestrian. That's a good word, Lydia." The girl beamed. "But I'm reading one right now and there's nothing pedestrian about it." The child resumed her pout. "Look," the mother said, "here's a *National Geographic*. You can learn all about the volcanoes of Hawaii." The girl rolled her eyes as if she'd been sentenced to counting sand on the beach, but she picked up the magazine and began thumbing through it.

Things grew quiet again, but it was only a few minutes until Alexa's first batch started spinning and she knew she would have to put it in the dryer soon. The woman had a batch set for a light wash that finished at about the same time, and so it was that Alexa found herself elbow-to-elbow with the other patron as they both unloaded their wash.

As they were beginning their work, the girl announced that Danny was poking her with a crayon, and the mother, still patient, made Danny move over two chairs.

"How old is she?" Alexa asked, breaking the ice.

"Eleven going on twenty-three," the woman answered. "Danny, keep the crayon to yourself or put it in the box."

"My baby sister is her age," Alexa observed. "Her name is Glorianna Celeste, but we all call her Annie."

"That's quite a handle for a kid."

Alexa shrugged. "Yeah. Mom seemed to think giving us pompous-sounding names would somehow make our fortunes." She smiled and offered her hand. "I'm Alexandra Cozette Babbidge, from Henderson, Kentucky, but my friends stick with Alexa."

"Lucretia Sherwood," the woman answered, accepting the proffered handshake. "Mom had the same idea, but friends call me Cretia for short."

"Lucretia," Alexa mused. "That's one my mother didn't think of."

Cretia smiled. "Are there many in your family?"

"Nine."

Lucretia looked confused for a moment. "No, I mean just your parents and brothers and sisters."

"Then it's eleven," Alexa answered.

Cretia's jaw dropped. "There are *nine children* in your family?"

"Yeah. I'm oldest, which is why I admire anyone who has your patience with half-grown kids." Alexa gestured toward the children. "You're really very good with them, you know."

"Thanks. I try."

Alexa examined her companion's hands, both full of wet laundry. Cretia wore a nice ring on the third finger of her right hand, but her left was bare. Although she knew better than to intrude, Alexa's native curiosity was on the prowl. "Single mother?" she asked.

Lucretia wiped her bangs from her eyes. "Yeah. You too?"

Alexa shook her head. "Never married."

"Smart girl." She continued to load wet clothing into a basket.

"You do have two lovely children to show for it, though," Alexa said.

Cretia stopped working and took a long breath. "Yeah, I do, don't I?" She smiled. "Of course, there are times when I wish I could dump them on their dad for a few hours, like when I do the laundry." She went back to loading clothes.

Alexa did too. "Dad's not involved?"

"Not much. He's supposed to take them on Thursday evenings and every other weekend, but he almost always seems to have a reason not to, like last Thursday when he just *had* to drive to Winslow to check out a car somebody was selling. If that means now what it meant when we were married, he probably didn't get home till the next morning."

Alexa softened her tone, aware she was prying. "Was the marriage rough?"

Cretia moved her cart toward the dryers and spoke in a more confidential tone, evidently not wanting the children to hear. "Yeah, it was. Of course, I thought I had the world by the tail in the beginning. Danny was a year older than I, the captain of the football team, the most popular guy in school. Everybody wanted to date him."

"Danny, like your son?"

"Yeah." She nodded toward the child. "He's Danny Junior."

"It sounds like things should have been great," Alexa coaxed.

"They probably should have been," Cretia continued, "except that we were both too young and Danny wasn't the least bit ready for marriage. He still isn't." She gave Alexa an apologetic frown. "You know the rest of the story: no education, no decent job, lots of frustration. When he was frustrated, he drank, and when he drank, he got mean. End of tale. Sorry if I bored you."

"Not at all," Alexa answered. "I'm interested in people. Besides, it's nice to meet someone local."

"How'd you come to be here anyway?" Cretia asked. Then it was Alexa's turn to tell the story of how she had arrived in Rainbow Rock. Though she never mentioned Kurt by name, she was careful to extol the virtues of the handsome cowboy who had rescued her on the road, then offered her temporary work.

"Sounds like you had a guardian angel on your shoulder," Cretia observed, and Alexa could only agree. "Think you can lend him, or her, to me for a while?"

"Sure," Alexa offered. "How long do you think you'll need him?"

Cretia's last washer was spinning now and the women were beginning to unload other clothes. "Just long enough to find a job. Danny's always late with child support, and housecleaning jobs are getting harder to come by as people get tight with their money."

Alexa could practically feel the light bulb going on

over her head. "A job, huh? What kind of work do you do?"

By the time the dryers had done their work and the women had their laundry folded, Alexa had made an appointment for Cretia to come by the office at ten the next morning.

"That's at Rainbow Productions?" Cretia asked, writing it down.

"Yeah, on Navajo Boulevard, near the corner of Hopi."

"Who's the owner?"

"Kurt McAllister and his sister-in-law, Meg."

"Aha!" Now the light was going on over Cretia's head. "When you started talking about the handsome blond hunk who rescued you, I should have put two and two together."

"You know Kurt?"

"Honey, around here, everybody knows everybody," Cretia answered, but she avoided Alexa's eyes and Alexa had an eerie feeling that something was going unsaid. "See you tomorrow at ten," she added as she steered the two children, and the bag full of clean laundry, back to her car.

"Yeah, see you." Alexa finished the more careful folding of her own things and packed them for the trip back to the car she had borrowed from Kate. If what she suspected was the case, there'd be some fireworks in the office tomorrow when she announced that Cretia Sherwood was coming in for an interview. Maybe that was just what Kurt needed to get his mind off her. She cringed, uneasily aware that part of her liked his attention. It was a part she would just have to squelch, she decided as she stepped into the howling storm.

* * *

The night wind was dying down and the sun just peaking the horizon when Kurt opened the office the next morning. Unable to sleep much past three A.M., he'd finally decided to go into the office to check the inventory on management tapes, in case he needed to run more copies of something before he and the ladies started work on their documentary. He also hoped some productive work would clear his mind of the images of Alexa that had been dancing through his vision all night, even in his sleep. Images? Heck, it was a veritable ballet. Whenever he closed his eyes, he saw Alexa—Alexa unconscious behind the wheel of her car, Alexa singing in his mother's parlor, Alexa laughing in the warm glow of the sunset, Alexa rising on tiptoe to brush her lips against his.

Amazing, what that brief kiss had done! He'd been kissed before. In fact, there'd been a few women who'd made it clear they planned to do much more than kiss, but nothing, *nothing* he'd experienced had ever packed the punch of that light touch. He'd almost persuaded himself that it was a fluke, or an indication that he'd been without female companionship too long. Eager to test his hypothesis, he'd planned to kiss her again when he drove her home Monday, but she'd dodged out of sight faster than a doe in deer season, leaving him to wait and wonder.

It was going to be torturous spending hours in the truck with her each day, driving to one interview after another and never having the opportunity to touch her or even talk as he wanted. As gun-shy as she was right now, he fully expected Alexa would place Meg in the middle seat between them. Well, he thought, he'd find out soon. Their schedule planned for them to drive to Chinle on Thursday.

Kurt opened the back room and began counting his inventory. By the time the sun was up and traffic was moving outside the studio, he'd not only counted everything in stock, but had already begun running copies of some of their more popular programs. He felt even better when he realized it'd been almost twenty minutes since he'd thought of Alexa.

Just as he thought her name, she came through the door, lovely as ever. A pair of dark-gray slacks emphasized her long legs and a rose-colored blouse hugged her curves becomingly. Her pale hair curved softly beneath her jaw and her blue eyes were alive with light. He, on the other hand, looked like boiled shoe-leather. He hadn't expected her this early. Though he'd showered before he left his house, he'd been planning on sneaking a shave in the office restroom before she arrived. "Morning," he called out, trying to sound cheery anyway, and absently rubbing his bewhiskered chin. "You're early."

"Morning," she answered, giving him a quick once-over that looked suspiciously like a comment on his grooming. "I had Chris give me a lift into town. I thought I'd get in early and finish editing your other videoscripts before we head out to the reservation on Thursday."

"Good thinking," Kurt answered, turning his back. He didn't want her to see how her mention of his brother's name rankled him.

They settled into a comfortable work pattern, Kurt copying and labeling videos, Alexa editing a proposed project on employee empowerment, her sling propped against the desk. Meg, who needed to stay off her feet these days, wasn't scheduled to come in until eleven or so. That looked to Kurt like a long, awkward morning. He reminded himself to slip away and catch that shave as soon as possible.

He was just about to make his escape when the phone rang and Alexa answered. "Good morning. Rainbow Productions," she said cheerily. He listened to see if he might need to answer, realized she was taking an order, and slipped away to do a careful and thorough shave. When he returned, she was just hanging up the phone.

"Good order?" he asked.

"Great order." Alexa had already been with the company long enough to know that bulk orders of more than ten were always a good sign. She named the client to Kurt, who whistled through his teeth.

"That *is* great news," he told her. "That company is strictly Fortune 500. We're breaking into the big time now!"

"With an order of fifty copies, no less." Alexa was beaming.

He was struck again by just how beautiful his companion was. Aloud he said, "We might just have to think of a way to celebrate. Do you have any plans for this evening?"

Alexa's smile faded, but only a little. "No, not really. . . ."

"Let's go out to dinner—you, me, Jim, and Meg. What do you say?"

Alexa hesitated, then said, "Sure, that sounds great."

"We're on, then. We'll schedule an exact time after

Meg comes in. I'll call Mom and let her know you won't be there for din—'' The phone rang again, interrupting him. It was another order, though not nearly so spectacular as the last. When Alexa hung up, Kurt picked up the extension on his desk. ''That last call reminded me. I'll call the paper right now to place a want ad.''

''Wait,'' Alexa interrupted. ''I think I may have found someone.''

''Oh, yeah?'' Kurt cradled the phone and stood. ''Tell me about it.''

So Alexa told him about taking her laundry out and meeting a young mother who was looking for a job. ''She's pleasant to talk to and has a nice voice,'' Alexa assured him, ''and I figured anybody who can be patient with a couple of preteen monsters could probably handle the kind of calls we get around here, so I invited her in for an interview.'' She hesitated, suddenly appearing unsure, and Kurt realized he was frowning. He tried to put on a happier face. ''I'm sorry if I overstepped my bounds,'' she went on. ''I didn't promise her a job or anything, just an interview.''

''No problem,'' Kurt assured her. ''It'll be great if she works out. Who is this person, anyway? If she's from around here, I probably know her.''

''Her name's Lucretia Sherwood,'' Alexa answered.

In the back of his awareness, Kurt knew that Alexa was watching him closely, gauging his reaction to her news, but he hardly noticed. He was concentrating on breathing; he felt as if a mule had just kicked him in the stomach. ''Holy Hannah,'' he mumbled under his breath, then sank into the closest chair.

''I gather you know her?''

"Yeah. I know her." Kurt passed a hand over his face. "Alexa, do you think you can keep an eye on the shop for a while?"

"Sure."

"I'll be back," he said, picking up his heavy coat. He turned back, not quite connecting with Alexa's eyes. "What time did you say she's coming in?"

"Ten o'clock."

"I'll be here." With that, he pulled on the coat and headed out the door. In just over an hour, Cretia Sherwood would be in his office, looking for a job. Worse yet, it was Alexa who had invited her. He didn't know if he could manage having the woman of his dreams and the one from his nightmares both sharing his space every day. "Coffee," he mumbled aloud. "I need coffee." Then he turned his boots toward the Kachina Café.

"Bingo," Alexa murmured as Kurt hit the door. So she had been right about Kurt and Cretia. She thought of how he'd looked when she came in this morning, more gorgeous than ever in his sexy morning beard. She thought of how he'd looked now, hearing Lucretia's name. Yes, there was definitely something here. She picked up the phone and dialed Meg. "Can you come in a little early?" she asked as Meg answered.

"Sure. Is there a problem?"

"Not a problem. It's just that we have a person interviewing for the receptionist position at ten. I assumed you'd want to be here."

"Good thinking. Sure, I'll be there. Who is this person, and how did this happen so quickly?"

Alexa answered the second question first with the

whole Laundromat story, then asked a question of her own. "Meg? When I tell you who it is that's interviewing, will you tell me why Kurt grabbed his coat and fled the building the moment he heard her name?"

There was silence on the other end of the line, then Meg gasped. "Not Cretia Sherwood!"

"This sounds interes—" Alexa began, but Meg cut her off.

"I'll be there in twenty minutes," she said, and hung up the phone.

This definitely sounds interesting, Alexa mused, wondering what she'd gotten them all into.

It was closer to fifteen minutes when Meg blew in through the back door, accompanied by a chilling, gusty breeze. " 'Morning," she murmured as she hung up her coat and scarf. Then she turned to Alexa with a no-nonsense look. "Okay, give me the whole rundown."

Feeling distinctly as if she was being grilled under hot lights, Alexa told the whole story, even repeating the scenes with the children. "I didn't realize they had a history," she apologized as she finished. "As I told Kurt, it's just an interview. You certainly don't have to hire her on my say."

"Forgive me if this sounds abrupt, Alexa, but we couldn't afford to hire anyone on your say. We will have to live and work with this person long after you've hit the big time in Hollywood."

Alexa felt the sting of Meg's censure. "I'm sorry. I've overstepped my bounds. I didn't mean to—"

"It's okay." Meg laid a gentle hand on Alexa's good arm. "We can certainly interview her." She sighed, settling back in her chair. "Who knows?

Maybe things have changed since . . ." She let the thought trail away.

"May I ask what happened?" Alexa ventured.

"You said she mentioned her divorce," Meg began. "How much did she tell you?"

"Enough that I know her ex got rough when he was drunk. It sounds like it got pretty bad."

"Yeah, I guess it did. Suffice to say their divorce kept the town talking for quite a while. It was fresh news when I came out from Walnut Creek—"

"That's when you met Jim?"

"Re-met is more like it. We were friends in high school."

"I didn't realize that."

"Yes, Jim and I were buddies and Danny Sherwood was my nemesis."

Alexa stiffened, feeling mildly nauseated. "I really have stirred things up, haven't I?"

"Yes, I'd say you have. Anyway, Cretia was freshly divorced and obviously looking for another husband. She wanted Jim at first . . ."

Alexa was feeling sicker by the minute. "So you don't have any reason to feel particularly kindly toward Cretia," she concluded.

Meg gave her a patient look. "Then when Jim married me, Cretia leveled her sights on Kurt."

Alexa moaned aloud. "I had no idea."

"I know you didn't. Things got pretty uncomfortable with Kurt and Cretia, but Kurt had the good sense to cut it off early. Then she turned her attention to his buddy, Rick." Meg sighed. "It was pathetic, really. Cretia's sense of self had been so battered that she seemed to feel worthless without a man to validate her.

She was subtle at first, but she was getting desperate. Rick had only taken her out a few times when she began acting as if they were a couple. It wasn't till he told her he wasn't interested anymore that she really got serious, then she was relentless. She even had her kids calling him 'Uncle Rick' and asking him to come for the weekend.''

''Oh, no.'' Alexa flinched.

''It went on for more than a year. Rick finally left town to get away from her, and Cretia packed up to follow him. That was when Kurt stopped her. He told her Rick would get a restraining order if she didn't leave him alone. I guess that was around a year ago.''

''I had no idea,'' Alexa repeated. She felt positively woozy. ''Look, I've got her phone number. Maybe I could call her and ask her not to come in. I can just tell her it was my mistake. That should take care of everything.''

Meg blew out a deep breath. ''No, I think we'd better see her. We can't afford a lawsuit at this point. Just do me a favor and don't schedule any more interviews without talking to one of us, okay?''

''You've got it,'' Alexa willingly agreed. She glanced at her watch. It was still forty minutes before ten. She wondered where Kurt was.

''And a piece of cherry pie,'' Kurt said as he watched the waitress refill his coffee cup. He instantly regretted his choice. Pie wasn't going to do anything to help the sick, empty feeling in his stomach. ''Cancel that pie,'' he grumbled. The waitress, who already had the plate in hand, gave him a disgruntled look, shrugged her shoulders, then put it back on the shelf.

Kurt took a deep breath and blew it out slowly. Cretia Sherwood. Of all the people for Alexa to meet! But what was done was done. He squared his shoulders. It was a quarter to ten. Time to face the music.

He crossed the street and sauntered up Hopi Boulevard toward the office, trying to compose both his face and his mind. *Don't be a wimp*, he counseled himself firmly. *She's just a woman—yeah, just a sad, pathetic, scared woman who wanted to make you or Rick responsible for all her troubles.* He blew out another deep breath. There was still Alexa to think of. It was too late to keep her from suspecting something, but with a little luck, he might be able to avoid involving her in it—at least, any more than she'd already involved herself. He reached his door, braced himself, and opened it.

Lucretia Sherwood was there, sitting at the front desk, looking for all the world as if she already ran the place. His first reaction was surprise at how good she looked. In the ten or eleven months since he'd seen her, she'd lost a few pounds, trimmed her hair, improved her wardrobe. She even looked less desperate, more . . . He hunted for a word . . . more *whole*. "Good morning, everyone," he said, trying to fasten his gaze on Meg, hoping she would see his unspoken cry and throw out a lifeline.

Bless her, she did. "Good morning, Kurt," she said. "I think everyone knows everyone, so we may as well get started." She indicated a chair—Kurt noticed it was the farthest from Cretia—and he sat in it, glad Meg was willing to run this show. Alexa sat in the background, watching curiously. He wondered what fallout there'd be with her when this charade was over.

Meg started with questions about Cretia's past work experience, interviewing her as if she were just another job applicant. Kurt listened to the answers, surprised at how clearly and confidently Cretia responded. He was surprised too to learn she had been working, cleaning homes for several clients on a regular basis. She'd come prepared with a list of references they could call. *That's new*, he contemplated. The Cretia Sherwood he had dated had been expecting him to support her and her children. Meg started asking about telephone skills and Kurt found himself chiming in, handing Cretia a product list and order form, then asking her to pick up the telephone as if it had just rung and conduct the conversation with him as the client. She did, handling the transaction as smoothly as if she'd been born to it, interrupting herself only to ask Meg if "Common Sense Leadership" came in closed-captioned. Half an hour later, Kurt had to admit this was a different woman from the one he'd expected. He also had to admit he was fairly impressed.

"Well, I think that's about it," Meg was saying, looking anxiously toward Kurt.

He took the cue, preparing to deliver the line he'd rehearsed. "Thank you for coming in, Ms. Sherwood. We have your number and we'll get back to you as soon as we've made a decision."

Cretia stood. "I have just one question, if I may."

Kurt, who had stood when she did, looked to Meg, swallowed, then said, "Yes?"

Cretia looked directly at Kurt. "I wonder if I might see you alone for a minute." She had called it a question, but it sounded more like a demand.

Meg said, "I don't think that's such a good—"

"Wait." Kurt cut her off. *No time like the present,* he told himself. "Sure, Cretia," he answered crisply. "We can step into the back room." He walked to the door and held it for her, then gave Meg a soulful look. The last thing he did was look at Alexa, wondering how all this would affect her—would affect them, if there was a "them" to affect.

He stepped into the back room and closed the door behind him. "Okay, Cretia. Let's have it."

Cretia stepped back, away from him. That was a relief. He had expected her to step much closer. "The job interview is really just an excuse to see you again," she said, and Kurt braced himself, trying to form a suitable answer that would let her know once and for all that he—"I've been wanting to talk to you. I need to apologize."

Kurt looked at her. What had she just said? "What did you just say?" he asked aloud.

"I need to apologize for all I put you through," she said. "You and Rick." Darned if she didn't sound sincere! "When I look back on all that, I'm very much ashamed of myself. It wasn't like me. I'd like to say it wasn't me at all," she paused, smiling wryly, "but I'm afraid there's too much evidence to the contrary." She sighed, turning away from him. "There are no excuses, really. I was alone with two young children to support and no job skills. I guess I got pretty desperate, but I'm sorry. I had no right to do that to either of you." She turned back around, facing Kurt, who hadn't spoken since she'd begun her spiel. "That last day, when you told me to stay away from Rick—" She blushed lightly. "I mean, when you finally made it plain, it was probably the kindest thing anyone has ever done for me.'' She cleared her throat uneasily. ''It was the first time I started thinking about making it, really making it work, on my own. I guess what I'm trying to say is, I'm sorry and I . . .'' She shrugged. ''Thank you. My life has been better since then.''

''I-I don't know what to say,'' Kurt stammered.

''You don't have to say anything. You don't even have to accept my apology, *or* my thanks. And believe me, I understand that you don't want to give me a job here. I just needed to say that.''

She stopped speaking and Kurt realized she had tears in her eyes—not forced, manipulative tears, either. A rush of understanding swept through him as he realized how much courage it had taken her to come here.

Lucretia straightened. ''Now, if you'll excuse me . . . ?'' She gestured toward the door.

Kurt leaned against it. ''Just a minute,'' he said, then swallowed hard. Was he sure he wanted to do this? And what would Meg think? He took a deep breath. ''Are you seriously interested in the job?''

Cretia's eyes widened. ''Yes. Absolutely! You don't mean to suggest you might consider . . .'' Her hopeful look was almost heartrending.

''It could be kind of uncomfortable.'' Kurt was amazed at his ability for understatement. ''But if you're willing to give it a try, I think we can use you. You understand it will be on a trial basis.''

Cretia blinked back tears. Kurt didn't know whether to feel like a hero or a heel. ''I'd like that very much,'' she said.

''It's a deal then.'' He offered his hand.

"A deal," she responded, soberly taking it in both of hers and giving him a look of sheer gratitude.

Kurt opened the door and stepped back into the office. "I think we have a new receptionist," he announced, then watched Meg's jaw drop halfway to the floor.

Chapter Four

It was brilliantly sunny on the reservation, and warmer than it had been, the sun beginning to melt a light runoff from the snowpack in the hills. Winter hovered near with the dark storm clouds that hung above the nearby peaks, and the wind was as high as ever, blowing dust and bits of last season's tumble-weeds across their path as they made their way up a rutted path outside of Chinle. Alexa sat on the right side of the cab with Meg on her left and Kurt driving. She was enchanted, staring out the window at a world she had never seen.

"It's magnificent," she said aloud. "Stark and barren, yet strikingly beautiful. I've heard people talk about the high desert all my life, but I've never seen anything like this."

"I know what you mean," Meg said. "Even when

58

I thought I didn't want to be here, I was always amazed by how beautiful it can be.''

"The one constant seems to be the wind," Alexa observed, then turned to her companions. "Does it always blow like this?"

"Ever since I've been here," Meg observed, "though I must admit it's worse in the spring."

"There's an old story," Kurt began, "about a pioneer fellow who came through here on his way to the gold fields in California. A few miles past Holbrook, his wagon broke down and he swore he'd fix it and move on as soon as the wind stopped blowing."

"And?" Alexa prompted, hearing a punch line coming.

"And they buried him in the Joseph City cemetery when he was ninety-four."

Alexa chuckled. "I guess you get used to it after a while."

"Not really," Meg answered, and Alexa chuckled again.

The past couple of days hadn't been as awkward as Alexa had expected, and they had certainly increased her admiration of Kurt. After what Meg had told her, Alexa was surprised that Kurt had allowed Lucretia an interview at all. Then there had been the quiet couple of minutes in the back room and Kurt had come out looking as serene as sunrise—and offering Cretia the job. He had been a considerate employer too, working out hours that fit the school schedule so Cretia could still manage her family, and helping her get acquainted in the business. Alexa, looking past Meg, cast him a curious glance. Kurt McAllister was a very kind person.

He had been a charming dinner companion as well. Their celebration with Jim and Meg had been one of the most enjoyable evenings Alexa had ever spent. Kurt had been full of interesting stories about the McAllister boys and Joan as children and about the early days of Rainbow Productions, but he had also been interested in her. He had asked about her background and had seemed impressed when she told of her graduate work at Columbia and how her instructors had introduced her to production houses that dealt with the networks in New York, creating her first opportunities to write for big-time TV. When Jim and Meg had left, excusing themselves so Meg could get off her feet, he had taken her dancing. Alexa had never imagined that a man of Kurt's size could move with such grace. If she closed her eyes, she could still remember what it had felt like to float around the dance floor in Kurt's arms, and she still suspected she'd cheated herself by dodging his kiss at the door. She smiled softly and glanced his way again. In the well-ordered plans she had made for her life, Kurt was a surprising complication.

They rounded a corner and came upon a scene that could have been five hundred years old—an eight-sided hogan perched below a hill, surrounded by tamarack bushes and rail corrals, a Navajo rug hanging over the door. "Looks like we've arrived," Kurt said, and stopped in the dooryard.

Alexa started to open her door. "Wait," Meg said, and put her hand on Alexa's arm.

They didn't have to wait long. A wrinkled old Navajo woman in a full-length satin skirt and velvet blouse came to the door, motioned toward the pickup, then retreated into the hogan, emerging moments later with four other women of varying ages, all similarly dressed. When they started toward the truck, Kurt opened his door and spoke to them, calling out a greeting Alexa didn't recognize.

"Now," Meg said, nodding to the door, and the two women got out the passenger side, walking around.

They joined Kurt about the same time as the five women did, and Kurt began the introductions, speaking first to the group of women, indicating Meg and Alexa. It wasn't until she'd been listening to him for several seconds that Alexa realized he was speaking in Navajo, and her admiration climbed several notches. Kurt turned to Meg and Alexa. "Ladies, I'd like you to meet Dorothy Bighorse. This is her home, and the other women are close relatives or clan members." He paused. "Meet Alice Chee, Helen Bitsilly, Dodie Billiman, and Lucille Tsosie. They're all weavers who have come to talk with us about their craft." Each woman nodded in acknowledgement as he introduced her. He turned and spoke again to the women. Dorothy responded in Navajo, adding an English "Welcome," and they started for the hogan.

There followed one of the most enlightening afternoons Alexa had ever spent. First was the hogan itself. What looked from the outside like a primitive earth dwelling was delightfully cool and pleasant inside, utilitarian but surprisingly inviting. Alexa barely had time to notice; she was soon busy taking notes on weaving. She managed to prop a clipboard against her sling and was then able to write with her right hand.

Dorothy had just completed a rug and was preparing to set up her loom for a new one. Kurt, who had come prepared with his Betacam and several blank tapes, caught it all on camera while translating the Navajo, getting help from the other Indian women when it came to weaving terms. Dorothy had a little English, which she used to help Meg and Alexa understand, and the other weavers added their varying language abilities to help clarify terms. Alexa watched the construction of the loom—this one set up outside the hogan under a spreading walnut tree—and worked madly to keep up with the conversation as the five talented crafters taught her the magic of warp and weft, the use of batten, shuttle, and heddle, and the intricacy of design.

Because the women were all of the Chinle area and worked in the traditional designs of that region, the rugs they had brought to show her were all of a similar make—banded, borderless patterns made in natural white, black, and gray wool and vegetal-dyed yarns in subtle earth tones of green, yellow, light brown, and beige. Yet despite their similarities, each rug was an individual work of art, as unique and fascinating as the woman who had given up weeks, or even months, of her life to create it.

Alexa learned too about other types of native textiles. Until this trip, she'd never realized that before the coming of white traders, Navajos wove or knitted all their clothing—shirts, skirts, mantles, shoulder blankets, and Mexican-style serapes, among other things, even belts and leggings. She was surprised to learn that knitting had been a traditional skill of Navajo men, that belts were often "free-woven" on an open loom, and that the art of weaving was almost a life-style in itself, complete with its own songs, traditions, and beliefs.

As the afternoon wore on, thunder rumbled low in the distance and the women began to talk about how it was raining heavily in the mountains, then Alice Chee questioned Dorothy about "getting the weaving sickness." When Kurt translated, Alexa asked for clarification. In English, Alice explained, "Some people just weave and weave and weave all the time and sometimes they think they might just weave their life away. That is the weaving sickness."

"I don't understand," Alexa said. "Can you explain more?"

Lucille spoke. "You get sick," she said, rubbing her body as if in pain. "You get sick in the arms, shoulders, and neck. It hurts you here and here."

"Oh, I see," Alexa said. "It's like when I work at my computer too long and my back and shoulders ache."

"Yes," Dorothy answered as lightning crackled in the distant hills, "and no, also. It's like when you're done with a blanket and you get a pain just below your neck, in here." She paused and indicated a space between her shoulder blades. "Its like needles sticking into you. That's the rug habit that does that to you."

"Or the arm you use for the batten may ache, or if you're tired all the time, or if you start not seeing the rug too well, then you know you've been weaving too much," Alice said. "That's the weaving sickness and you need a ceremony."

"A ceremony?" Alexa asked, pen in hand.

"There is a ceremony," Helen explained, "for

when someone weaves too much. They grind the white or yellow corn and just put all the weaving tools in it. They use the Blessingway, the *hózhóójí*.''

''It takes a long time sometimes,'' Alice interrupted, as Alexa listened in fascination. ''Each medicine man sings his own version of the spinning song. Then they all sing the grinding song, and then another song from the Blessingway, called 'Beauty Around You.' ''

''You always use the Blessingway for weaving sickness,'' Dodie continued. ''All the *yodi bighiin*—'' She turned to her companions. ''How do you say that in English?'' They debated for a moment until Kurt translated the term as ''Soft-Goods Songs.'' ''Yes,'' Dodie went on, ''all the Soft-Goods Songs are sung over the one who is sick from too much weaving: 'The Sheep Song,' 'The Weaving Song,' 'The Grinding Song,' 'The Spinning Song,' 'The Beans-of-Four Colors Song' . . . They sing all the things for women.''

''So weaving is always a woman's craft?'' Alexa asked, and the women discussed it among themselves, then nodded in agreement.

Alexa shook her head in amusement. Her friends at Columbia wouldn't know how to deal with a culture that still divided all its most significant activities by gender. ''What if a woman is sick of too much weaving,'' she asked, trying to pick up the phrase the women had used, ''and she can't get people together for a Blessingway?''

The women considered her question while Kurt flashed her a smile that approved her astuteness, then Lucille answered. ''If ever you are sick of too much weaving and you don't have money enough for a Blessingway ceremony, you can just take all the pieces you brush off the weaving and put them on a burning coal and breathe in the smoke, then rub it on your arms and hands. Just massage it in.''

''I do that to keep the weaving sickness from coming,'' Dorothy answered.

''As a preventive, you mean?'' Meg interjected, and Kurt translated.

Dorothy nodded in response. ''Now when I finish a rug I just sweep up all the pieces of yarn with my hand, and burn them in the stove. That way there is never weaving sickness.''

''There are other ways to stop the weaving sickness from coming,'' Alice added. ''Weaving should be done with care, with . . .'' She asked Kurt for a word and he responded, ''moderation.'' ''Yes,'' she said, ''with moderation. Overdone weaving is *ak'éitl'o*. It can be remedied by a sacrifice to the *beedizi*, the spindle.'' The women chattered briefly, then Dorothy went inside and brought out a prayerstick that consisted of yucca, precious stones, bird and turkey feathers, and tassels of grass and pollen. ''You use this as part of the blessing rite,'' she explained as she showed Alexa the parts. ''You recite the prayer to the gods when you make the sacrifice.''

The women all nodded their approval. ''There is one other way,'' Helen added. ''Never make a rug with a border.'' Again, the women nodded.

''But I've seen some nice rugs with borders,'' Meg stated. ''Are all those weavers in danger of the weaving sickness?''

''Yes,'' Dodie answered soberly, ''unless they make a pathway.''

''Pathway? Tell me more about the pathway,'' Alexa prompted, but the women shook their heads and spoke to one another in Navajo.

"They say they cannot tell you much about the pathway," Kurt translated, "because none of them practice it. They all make only borderless rugs. Helen says there are other weavers who are experts on the pathway. We'll be talking to them later."

"I'll look forward to that," Alexa answered, hoping it would happen before she left for California. She was surprised how much she was enjoying this assignment.

"We got some great stuff today," she said to Kurt as they returned in the pickup later that evening. They were talking over Meg, who was ignoring them and trying to doze.

"Yeah, I think this will add a nice dimension to our finished piece."

"Especially the stuff about the weaving sickness and how you have to cure it. Can you tell me more about the Blessingway and the idea of a ceremony? I mean, what they were talking about sounded like simple repetitive-motion injury. Why not just take two aspirin and get a good night's sleep?"

"That's a big question and a little tough to answer," Kurt said. "Anything I say will surely oversimplify a very complex idea. Essentially the Navajos believe in a whole, integrated world. All things are a part of it and have their place in it, including humans and human activities."

"So far, so good," Alexa answered. "That seems like a healthy concept I've heard before."

"Here's where it diverges," Kurt went on. "Whenever a human being experiences illness—of the body or the mind—it comes from being out of place, out of sync, so to speak, with the rest of the natural world. A ceremony is designed to bring the person back to wholeness, back to rightness with the rest of everything.''

''Have you ever seen a ceremony?''

''Yes, I've seen one complete ceremony, but you have to realize they're off-limits to most *belagaana*—''

''Most what?''

''Outsiders like you and me.''

''Then how did you come to see it? And how did you learn to speak Navajo, anyway?''

So Kurt told her about the couple his father had hired when Jim was a new baby and how the McAllister children had grown up with Ruth and Franklin Nakai and their growing boys. ''Ruth helped Mom in the house and although she understood English, she preferred not to speak it, so most of us grew up speaking English to our mother and Navajo to Ruth. It's pretty much a native tongue with us.''

''Well, I'm impressed,'' Alexa said. ''It sounds like it would be a very difficult language to learn.''

''I'm told the only way to learn it with any level of mastery is to learn it natively. For one thing, it's tonal, and most Anglo ears can't even distinguish among words that are totally different to a Navajo. Jim is really much better at it than I am, because he uses it so often.''

''But about the ceremony,'' Alexa prompted.

''The one I saw occurred when we were little, so I don't remember much. Jim and Chris and I were staying with the Nakai children's grandmother on the reservation. Her name is Clara Begay,'' he interrupted himself. "She's an expert weaver we may interview later. Anyway, Jim and I were out riding and his pony caught a gopher hole and rolled, pinning Jim's leg under him. It was a crushing injury, and seemed pretty bad. *'Ama-sani* said we'd need a ceremony.''

"Who said?"

" '*Ama-sani*. It's what we sometimes call Clara. It means grandmother.''

"So she had a ceremony for Jim?"

"I'm not sure what kind. Jim was about ten, so I guess I wasn't much older than six. All I remember clearly was that she hired a singer to come to her summer hogan.''

"A singer is a medicine man?"

"One of the most respected types. This singer must have carried some heavy weight among the people because Clara Begay is known and loved by just about everybody. I don't even think he charged her much. Anyway, it was a short ceremony—only two days and a night.''

Alexa's eyes widened. "That's short?"

"I'm told the Beautyway goes for nine full days.'' His brow furrowed. "Or is it the Night Chant?'' He shook his head. "Anyway, some of them are really impressive.''

"Wow.''

"Wow is right. Mostly I remember that night. Just after sundown, the man began singing. The songs are always elaborate. I'm told a singer has to memorize them all perfectly before he's allowed to perform the ritual, right down to inflection and gesture. It can take years.'' Kurt paused and downshifted. Meg stirred and he eased back on the gas to let her rest better. It was a small thing, but it touched Alexa to see him do it.

"As I said," he continued, "it started just after sundown, and as the man sang, he spread colored sands upon the floor of the hogan, depicting the *yei*, or holy people, and other holy signs in a circular pattern."

"Like some of the sand paintings you see in the curio shops in New Mexico."

Kurt smirked. "Yes, only the sand paintings in the curio shops aren't much like the real sand paintings done in ceremonies," he said. "The ones you've seen are created strictly for tourists. A real sand painting is always done by a professional singer, always on the floor of the hogan where the sing takes place, always started after the sun goes down, and is destroyed—the colored sands scattered widely—before dawn."

"Destroyed? Why?"

"The Navajos believe only the *yei* can produce perfection. Since human representations of holy things are necessarily imperfect, they must always be undone."

"I had no idea," Alexa said. "It's a very complicated art, isn't it?"

"At least as complicated as weaving," Kurt answered. "In the one I saw, the man took hours to perfect the sand painting, singing the whole time, then when it was finished, he sat Jim down in the middle of it and began applying parts of the painting to his body, mostly to his injured leg, but also to his head and chest and back. He was using the power of the holy pictures to cure Jim."

Alexa shook her head. "It sounds so . . ." She searched for a word.

"Primitive? Childlike? Nonscientific?"

"Well, yeah."

"That's the way most outsiders react to it," Kurt said, looking quickly at Meg, who had just moaned in her sleep. "But you have to realize, Navajo medicine men had been practicing cures for centuries before they ever heard of white medicine. Many of them are expert herbalists, most can set a bone as well as any Anglo doctor—at least, without surgery—and they're excellent practitioners of wellness, trying to keep people whole and healthy so there's little need for healing ritual."

"But these ceremonies . . . How can rubbing some colored sand on a boy's leg cure a crushing injury?"

Kurt's brows drew together in concentration. "Let me see if I can explain," he said, then paused to negotiate a place where snow runoff flooded the road. "One of the aspects of human health that Western medicine frequently ignores is the psyche. Anglo doctors tend to treat pathologies, only becoming involved with a patient after symptoms are presenting, and usually by hitting those symptoms with chemicals or surgical procedures. They rarely look at the psychic phenomena that accompany the illness or injury."

It occurred to Alexa that she may just have been transported into the Twilight Zone. "What do you mean by psychic phenomena?"

"You're injured, right? And you worry about it. Is it going to be okay? Will you ever walk on that leg again? Is this illness just a sign of something a lot worse? Does the pain suggest something really bad is wrong?"

Alexa nodded. "I see what you mean."

"A sing takes care of that. You spend hours, sometimes days, with the people you love all gathered around you, all directing their primary attention to healing you, spending their scant resources to have a doctor treat you. The doctor sings a ceremony that gives you comfort and ensures you are part of the universe, then he assures you that your life is back in harmony again.''

"No more worries," Alexa said, understanding.

"No more worries," Kurt agreed. "Navajo medicine men are excellent psychiatrists, when you think about it."

"I can see that," she answered, her respect for ancient ways increasing.

Meg stirred and moaned again. Kurt gave her a worried look.

"Do you think she's all right?" Alexa asked. "She seems awfully pale."

"I don't know. It's the sounds she makes that concern me, and she seems to be sleeping more deeply than I'd have thought possible."

"Maybe I should try to wake her?"

Kurt seemed undecided. "I hate to. She tires so easily lately. Still, I'd hate to think something is really wrong."

Alexa smiled wryly. "There we go, huh? Adding worry to a condition to make it worse."

"Exactly," Kurt agreed, smiling. "We could probably use a sing."

"I'm going to try to wake her," Alexa said, then gently shook Meg's arm. "Meg? Meg?" She shook harder. "Wake up, Meg."

Meg moaned, but didn't awaken. She looked paler than ever.

Alexa, becoming alarmed, shook her hard. "Meg, wake up!" Kurt joined in, grabbing her knee and shaking it, calling her name as loudly as Alexa was. Meg moaned again and opened her eyes.

"Are you okay?" Kurt asked.

"I think I'm just tired," Meg began, then she paused on a sudden intake of breath. "Oh, that hurts!" She hugged herself protectively around the widest part of her girth.

"Meg, what's happening?" Kurt asked.

"I don't know. I think it's the baby. How much farther, Kurt?"

"Probably thirty miles." Kurt tromped on the accelerator. "The roads are sloppy with runoff, but I'll get you there as quickly as I can. Alexa, use the cell phone. Call Jim and tell him what's happening. Then I'll give you the number for the clinic." Alexa, pale now herself, followed Kurt's instructions. "Take it easy, Meg," he said, patting her arm. "We're going to take good care of you." Then he looked skyward and mumbled something about the approaching rain. "Just pray it doesn't get any closer," he said.

Meg winced. Alexa gripped her hand and murmured a quiet prayer.

Kurt paced the foyer of the Holbrook clinic, as nervous as any expectant father. It had been more than an hour since their hurried arrival. Jim had met them at the door and Dr. Kemp had taken Meg right in. The doctor had gone in and out a couple of times, smiling reassurance but tight-lipped, never stopping to hear or answer questions. Kurt turned to look at Alexa. She was pale and clearly distressed, but still beautiful. It amazed him that no matter what the circumstances, Alexa was always beautiful.

He paced and reviewed the week. Until Meg's condition became worrisome, it had been fairly successful. He was surprised to see how well Cretia was working out. She'd adapted to the job immediately, and both he and Meg had been amazed to see how many more orders they took when someone was there to answer the phones. They'd done well enough with the order line and one of them occasionally picking up phones. It hadn't occurred to them that they might be missing substantial business just by not having a receptionist. Now it was beginning to look like the difference in orders would more than pay Lucretia's salary, especially since they'd just picked up a second Fortune 500 company as a client.

Meg had also managed well his high-handedness in hiring Lucretia. Though she had taken him aside to remind him that she was a full partner in the business and he ought to consult her on such matters, her real concern had been to make sure that Cretia wasn't blackmailing him in some way. But she wasn't. The desperate, dependent woman he had once learned to dread hadn't shown her face once all week. Cretia's behavior had been entirely professional and above reproach. Though he was still vaguely distrustful of what might come next, Kurt was grateful that he'd gone with his gut instinct and given Cretia the chance. He'd have to remember that he owed Meg one.

He was also pleased with his progress with Alexa. She was still determined to head for Burbank at the end of the next month, but she was spending less time with Chris and more with him. When he'd taken her dancing last Tuesday after Meg and Jim went home, she'd melted against him like butter on warm toast. It was enough to encourage a man, and Kurt was already easily encouraged when it came to a certain beautiful blond with eyes like the summer sky. He just wished she'd stop dodging his kisses.

The office intercom on the receptionist's desk buzzed and Myra picked it up with a murmured "Yes?" then turned to Kurt. "You two can go in now."

Alexa was on her feet in an instant and by Kurt's side. She looked wide-eyed and worried, and he gave her what he hoped was an encouraging smile, then took her hand as they walked together down the hall to examining room three. "Somehow this all seems familiar," Kurt said.

"Too familiar," Alexa agreed as they entered the room.

Meg was stretched full-length on the examining table, propped up with pillows at her back but looking slightly less pale. Jim sat beside her on a stool. Dr. Kemp stood at her feet, making notes on a chart. "Well, folks, we've had quite a scare here," he said, adding a note or two before he put the chart down, "but it looks like everything is under control."

"Thank heaven," Kurt said with a sigh. "What happened?"

"The doctor thinks I just got overtired," Meg said, but Dr. Kemp quickly disagreed.

"No, young lady. It's more complicated than that. You started labor out there on the reservation." He turned to Kurt and Alexa. "We had to use drugs to stop the contractions. I'm just glad you weren't farther away.''

"Would the baby stand a chance if it were born now?" Kurt asked the doctor.

"Yes, it would stand a good chance, but there would still be considerable risks. The little one is much safer where it is for at least another month, and six weeks would be even better.''

"So what does this mean?" Kurt continued.

Jim answered. "It means my wife is going to have to take it easy for a couple of months," he said sternly. "No out-of-town travel, no long days, and she's off her feet and down for the day the first time she has two contractions in a row. Right, Meg?"

Meg gave a put-upon sigh. "Yes, dear."

Jim looked up triumphantly. "You're both witnesses," he said. "She'll probably never say that again in her life.''

Alexa smiled softly—Kurt thought it was that dawn-on-the-desert smile again—and took Meg's hand. "I'm glad you're going to be okay, Meg."

"Do you think you can hold down the fort, production-wise?" Meg asked her. "I mean, until you have to leave for Burbank.''

"Sure, I'll be glad to," Alexa said, patting Meg's hand.

"Well, enough of this," the doctor ordered. "Get this pregnant lady home to bed.''

"Yes, Doctor," Jim said. "Come on, wife."

"You may have to help me out to the car," Meg said. "I'm still kind of shaky on my feet.''

"No problem," Jim said, and lifted her into his arms.

"Jim! Put me down! I'll hurt your back, you numb-skull."

Jim grinned and held his wife close. "Get the door for me, will you, bro?"

"Sure thing," Kurt answered.

"Oh, and Kurt, thanks for getting her here safely."

Kurt nodded. "My pleasure, though I wondered if we'd outrun the rain."

"Looks like it didn't get this far," Jim said, settling his wife in his pickup. "But it's been wild in the mountains. I'll bet Grand Falls is running."

"I expect so." Kurt paused. "Well, take care of our lady, brother."

"You bet I will."

Minutes later, Kurt and Alexa were pulling up behind the office where they planned to put away the equipment and organize their notes before quitting for the day. Kurt had already checked in with his mother to let her know Meg was well, and she'd warned him there wasn't much in supper leftovers. It seemed like an opportunity.

"May I buy you dinner before I take you home?" he asked as they sorted equipment and put it all away carefully.

"Sure, I'd like that."

"That'll be great," he said. "Do you like Thai? We have a great Thai restaurant in town."

"I love Thai," Alexa answered.

"That's what we'll do then." Kurt noticed the stack of messages on Cretia's desk. "Do you want to check the messages? See if there's anything we need to handle before we leave?"

"Sure." Alexa went to the spindle and began filing

through them. "Ah, here's an interesting one. The garage called. My car is ready."

"We can pick it up during lunch tomorrow. I'll drive you." He noticed the worried expression on Alexa's face. "Something wrong?"

"Not really," she said, shaking off his concern.

"You're worrying about whether you can afford it," he guessed.

"I didn't plan enough money for major repairs," she answered.

He walked up behind her and put both hands on her shoulders. "Don't worry, Alexa. This will all work out."

She turned and smiled up at him, another of those breathtaking, dawn-breaking smiles, and Kurt knew the moment had come. He leaned toward her, preparing to test his kiss hypothesis. Alexa's eyes drifted closed—and she sneezed dramatically!

"Oh Kurt, I'm sorry!" she said. "I think there must have been dust on the message slips. I just—" She sneezed again.

"That's okay," he said, only slightly discouraged.

But the mood was broken and Alexa seemed eager to take advantage of the change. "I think I'm going to sneeze again," she said. "Excuse me?" She slipped away, sneezing loudly, and hurried into the bathroom.

Kurt watched her go, shaking his head with a sigh. Life was *not* fair!

Chapter Five

Alexa had always loved Fridays. Some of that was the usual TGIF, but not much. She enjoyed her work and seldom found herself ticking down the moments until her escape. No, she loved Fridays because she relished the sense of wholeness that came with the end of a productive work week. As a writer, she liked cliff-hangers too, so she always tried to start something new on Friday that would beckon her back, excited to see Monday come.

This Friday offered the promise of both. It was also, Alexa observed as she entered the office at Rainbow Productions, the last time she would have to beg a ride from Chris to get to work. Before the day ended, she'd be back in her own wheels.

The only obstacles that stood in the way this par-ticular Friday were the wisps of dream that hung like loose threads about the edges of her day. Her writer's mind generally dreamed in vivid detail and in living color, and last night's dreams had been of Kurt. She had seen him sitting at the loom, his beautifully structured back to her, his strong hands weaving a lovely banded rug—only the pattern in the middle was her face. Later, after she had shaken the image and had slipped back into sleep, her dreams had gone from Grade B horror film to sitcom farce.

Her later dreams had reenacted their brief kiss on the porch, only this time there were repeated kisses— one after the other, all meltingly delicious, and few of them brief. Behind them on the porch stood a boxcar-sized Kiss-o-Meter whose dial shot off sparkling Roman candles each time Kurt's lips brushed hers.

She had awakened with Kurt's image in her mind, her body still tingling from the imagined touch of his hands at her waist, back, and shoulders, her mouth still hungry for another of those toe-curling, mind-rattling, Kiss-o-Meter-blowing kisses.

Alexandra Cozette, it's time to get your mind on your work, she chided herself. Convinced her mother couldn't have said it better, she settled at her desk and positioned her left arm, still in its sling, so it would rest on the desktop. She was picking up yesterday's notes when Kurt sidled in.

"Starting early?" he asked, cocking one eyebrow.

Heavens, he was gorgeous! He wore jeans and a blue chambray shirt, boots, and a gray Stetson. Alexa realized with a jolt that he'd been wearing jeans and blue chambray when she'd last seen him—in front of the Kiss-o-Meter.

"I, uh, I thought I'd look over my notes before we do this morning's interview in the studio." Alexa felt the same sensation she always did whenever she and Kurt were alone, as if he were the sun and she a wandering body being drawn through the heavens into his orbit. It would be just the two of them, and Cretia, in the office today since Meg was under doctor's orders to stay off her feet through the weekend. She wondered if she'd make it to lunch without falling all over him.

"You seemed to get into the talk yesterday," Kurt said. He was watching her with a look so intense that it seemed to be weaving itself about her, drawing her into the pattern of his life.

Her face warmed and her stomach tightened. "Yes," she answered weakly, then with greater strength, "yes, I did enjoy it. I'd never thought much about weaving until we started this project. Now I can hardly wait to learn more."

"The guy we're interviewing here this morning has an interesting perspective," Kurt began. "He's been a trader for the last thirty years." As they went to work side by side, preparing the studio and setting up lights and cameras, the intensity about them slowly dissipated.

But it was never really gone. While trading post owner Garland McGee unreeled his knowledge of Navajo rugs before Kurt's Betacam, the magical spell swirled about them. A half dozen times Alexa spoke a question, only to hear the same words come out of Kurt's mouth. As often as she looked up, Kurt was watching her, and the potent power of his gaze drew her with almost hypnotic force. Sometimes she had to look away, catch her breath, then ask the trader to repeat himself.

Near the end of the interview, McGee drew out the rugs he had brought as examples, and finally got Alexa's full attention. "Certain styles or patterns developed around different trading posts," McGee explained as he spread an elaborate bordered rug for the camera. "Various traders encouraged styles they especially liked or could get more money for, and weavers in that area perfected that style. This one is from the Teec Nos Pos region, up by Red Mesa. The style developed around 1930. Notice the soft earth colors contrasted with flat black in the border, and the pattern—very elaborate in the interior with a repeating pattern in the border." Alexa took notes while Kurt shot footage of the rug from various angles.

"The Two Gray Hills design is similar," McGee went on as he spread another rug next to the first. "These rugs are especially known for the fineness of their weave. They use natural colors almost exclusively—gray, some beige or tan, white, and black—and these rugs are elaborately patterned and bordered. The patterns tend to be larger and more traditional in the Two Gray Hills rugs. This style developed first—it was known by 1925—and many people think it influenced the Teec Nos Pos pattern. Others believe both were influenced by the popularity of Oriental rugs at that time. Native weavers apparently tried to copy what was selling well among their Anglo clients."

"That second rug definitely has an Oriental look," Alexa observed.

"But the patterns are still traditional Navajo," McGee said, unrolling a third rug. "This pattern also developed around Red Mesa. It copies a nineteenth-century style known as an eyedazzler."

"Wow." Alexa felt tempted to rub her eyes. "I can see why." Brilliant reds and yellows mixed with rich dark brown in crisscross patterns with sharply serrated edges. The effect was indeed dazzling.

McGee went on to show them several bordered Crystal rugs, developed for J. B. Moore's Crystal Trading Post; an unusual borderless Ganado rug that featured large, square "Hubbell crosses," so named because trader J. L. Hubbell had encouraged revival of the classic pattern; a borderless Wide Ruins rug in vegetal-dyed green and brown striping patterns; and a bordered Burntwater in beige, brown, yellow, and rust.

"Here are two more from the Ganado-Klagetoh area," he said, spreading the two side by side over the other rugs that already littered the studio floor. "These are more typical of that region. Notice the heavy borders and the mix of bright red with natural white, black, and gray."

Alexa stroked the fine weave of the nearer rug. "These are more like what I think of when I picture Navajo rugs," she said. "They're beautiful."

"Yes, they certainly are that," McGee agreed. He showed them a pair of borderless, striped Chinle rugs like those Alexa had seen the day before at the hogan of Dorothy Bighorse, then he said, "The only major styles we haven't seen yet are the storm pattern and the pictorials."

"Pictorials, as in pictures?" Alexa asked.

"That's right, but here, let's look at the storm pattern first. Grab that corner, will you?"

Alexa helped him roll out a beautiful rug about three by four feet. It was bordered and woven in red, tan, black, and gray, with a striking pattern in near-white wool. The pattern featured a large rectangle at the center of the blanket with a black-and-red figure at its center. White yarn in serrated lines went outward from the corners of the central rectangle to other rectangles in each of the rug's four corners, and each rectangle contained a smaller shape like the one in the center.

"What's the pattern?" Alexa asked. "It almost looks like a stylized human figure."

"That's as good a guess as anyone's," McGee answered. "Some people believe the style is sacred. They say the central pattern represents a hogan and the smaller ones in the corners are the four sacred mountains of *Dinehtah*—"

"Excuse me? Of what?"

"*Dinehtah*," Kurt answered before McGee could. "Navajoland. Navajos call themselves *Dínéh*, the people. The place where they live is *Dinehtah*."

"The connecting lines between them are supposed to be lightning bolts," McGee went on. "They carry blessings from the sacred mountains to the people." Then he shrugged. "Other people think Moore invented the pattern himself, then came up with the story to do some creative marketing. The style, featured in his 1911 catalog, was developed on the western side of the reservation, around Tuba City."

"Fascinating," Alexa answered, taking notes as rapidly as she could. "That just leaves the pictorials, right?"

"Right," McGee said. "Of course, there are many variations on each of the styles we've seen, but there are probably more variations on the pictorial than on anything else. Since the rugs show pictures, they can be of almost anything. Take this one, for instance.''

Another rug was rolled out over the others. Rectangular and borderless, it featured a variety of birds and animals in serrated white frames. Flowering vines wound their way among the pictures, all in brilliant synthetic colors. ''Wow,'' said Alexa. ''This can't be a traditional style, can it?''

''No, this one is very contemporary,'' McGee answered, ''but here's something very traditional.'' He rolled out a square, borderless rug with a flat brown background. On it were elaborate symbols in the shape of a cross, a squared ''U'' of brightly colored lines winding partway around it. ''This depicts a sand painting.''

Alexa's eyes widened. ''A real sand painting? A holy pattern?''

''Exactly. This one probably shows the Windway ceremony, bordered on three sides by the Rainbow Goddess.''

''The Rainbow Goddess,'' she repeated, touching the arcing band of color. ''But do they allow . . . I mean, is it okay for Navajos to depict these sacred ceremonies to outsiders?''

McGee smiled approvingly. ''I see you understand something of the religion.''

''A little.'' Alexa flashed Kurt a grateful smile, which he promptly returned.

''The first depiction of holy symbols in a rug was woven in 1896 by a woman whose name is now lost to history. She pictured one of the Yei.''

Alexa looked to Kurt. ''One of the holy people,'' he said.

"Yes, one of the holy people," McGee continued. "Navajos all over the reservation waited, expecting her to die, or at least go blind. When she didn't, the people reasoned that perhaps the Yei didn't mind. The first sand-painting blanket, like this one, was done by a man named Hosteen Klah in 1925."

Alexa, her eyes turned to her notes, began waving her hand. "Wait. A *man* did the first sand-painting pattern?"

"Yes, and Hosteen Klah soon became one of the biggest names in weaving. His nieces all adapted the style, being careful never to quite finish a pattern, out of respect for the Yei, and they rapidly became well-known also." He paused and rolled out two more rugs. "The last two examples depict the Yei and the *yei-bichai*."

Alexa, scribbling like mad, stalled on the last word. "The what?"

"The *yeibichai*," Kurt answered. "The Yei are the holy people, and the *yeibichai* are mortal Navajos who impersonate them in sacred dances."

"You can tell the difference," McGee explained, "because the Yei are always highly stylized and generally pictured in frontal view. *Yeibichai* are more human-looking, always fully dressed in traditional clothing, and almost always pictured in side view."

"I see," Alexa said, still writing as fast as she could. In the rugs, the difference was clear.

McGee talked for a while longer, about how the Yei rugs developed near Shiprock differed from the coarser, large-weave Yei rugs from the region around Lukachukai and Upper Greasewood, about how some modern pictorials included objects such as cars and telephone poles, about weavers such as Daisy Taugel-chee, Sadie Curtiss, Philomena Yazzie, and Agnes Smith who could command many thousands of dollars for a rug before it was even started. Alexa found it all fascinating.

But there was one question he hadn't answered. As he rolled up his rugs and prepared to leave, Alexa asked, "You've shown us lots of rugs with borders. The weavers we met yesterday said one should never weave a bordered rug unless it has a pathway. Can you tell me more about that?"

"Oh, you mean the Spirit Trail," McGee said. "Unfortunately, I don't have an example, but the Spirit Trail is just a break in the border. Sometimes it's woven into the pattern, sometimes it's just a thread through the edge. They tell me some trails are even invisible except to the weaver herself. It's the way the *chindi*, the evil spirits, get out of the rug. Sometimes it's called the Devil's Path."

"Evil spirits?" Alexa repeated, eyes wide. "Devils?"

"Yeah, that's what I said. Apparently the weaver believes she'll get sick if she doesn't let the evil spirits out."

"I've heard of the weaving sickness. Can you tell me more about it?"

"That's about all I know," McGee answered. "There are some weavers who still use the Spirit Trail, though. You might ask them."

"We will," Kurt assured the trader as he left.

By the time McGee closed the front door behind him, Alexa was fairly bursting with enthusiasm for the project, and that enthusiasm gave her something impersonal, something safe she could discuss with Kurt. "Evil spirits!" she said as they left together, using their lunch break to go after her car. "Do you think anybody will believe this if we put it on tape?"

"You might not want to take that as gospel," Kurt said as he helped her into the cab of his truck. "McGee knows a lot about the history of Navajo weaving and he's very up on regional patterns, but I'm not sure he knows his stuff when it comes to the pathway. We're interviewing Jim on camera this afternoon, though. Maybe you can ask him about it."

"I will," Alexa promised.

The garage had done a thorough job with her car. Alexa thought it looked better than before the accident. The mechanics had already dealt with the insurance company and most of the cost of repairs had been covered, less her deductible. She hated to see Kurt write a check for the rest. The odd tension that always stretched between them when they were alone together made her loath to owe him any more. Still, Kurt assured her as he always did that she was worth far more to Rainbow Productions than she was costing him. Alexa still noted the amount in her checkbook, promising to repay it all.

They had a quick lunch at the Kachina Café, then hurried back to the studio, Alexa driving one-handed because of the sling, but still behind the wheel of her own car for the first time in more than a week. They barely had time to set up again before Jim arrived. He had nothing but good to report about Meg's condition, and they were soon ready to go on camera.

Alexa was amazed at the range of Jim's knowledge. Like McGee, he seemed loaded with facts about Navajo life. He echoed much of what McGee had said about regional styles, then showed a pair of "eyedazzlers" that were more jarring than dazzling. He named the early traders Moore and Hubbell, then went on to mention others—C. N. Cotton, Richard Wetherill, and the Lippincotts. He told of a period when native weavers were asked to use the brightly colored, synthetically dyed yarns from mills around Germantown, Pennsylvania, then displayed an antique Germantown rug from the late 1880s. "Rising demand at the turn of the century led to a drop in quality," he told them, "sometimes even to woolen rugs woven on cotton warp. That in turn led to a glutted market and falling prices, which circled back to a demand for higher quality and resulting higher prices."

"Many reputable weavers now won't touch yarn they haven't prepared and dyed themselves," he concluded. "Often they won't use a dye they haven't made themselves, unless a trusted family member made it."

"Except for Ganado weavers," Kurt interrupted.

"That's true," Jim answered. "In some areas—Ganado is one example—it has become 'traditional' for the weavers to use synthetically dyed colors, like the brilliant Ganado red. Still, it's true that most native weavers prefer the vegetal dyes."

"Do you know weavers who can show us how to make natural dyes?" Alexa asked. Her hand was beginning to ache from all the notes she had so eagerly taken.

"Several, including some that are on your schedule," Jim answered. He went on to discuss weaving techniques: the plain weave, in which both warp and weft are visible; the more common tapestry weave, in which the weft threads—sometimes as many as a hundred per square inch—completely cover the warp; and the pulled-warp or wedge-weave, popular during the 1870s but rarely used since, in which the warp was woven at a diagonal to create a zigzag pattern.

When he seemed to be winding down, Alexa asked about the Spirit Trail. "Ah, there's a concept," Jim said, apparently relishing the idea as much as Alexa did. "Here, I've got one rug that has a pathway. Let me show it to you." He rolled out a lovely bordered rug in a Ganado pattern, then showed Alexa a place near the top right corner where a thread from the interior gray design ran through the edge of the black border. He followed the thin gray line with his finger. "Here it is."

"It almost looks like a flaw in the design," Alexa said.

"Many early traders thought that's what it was. They paid less for rugs with 'flaws' in them, so the incidence of pathways in the rugs dropped off dramatically. Since the rise in quality, more knowledgeable traders sometimes pay more for a rug with a pathway."

"But what about the belief?" Alexa asked. "If it's a trail to let evil spirits out, don't all rugs need one? Or don't all weavers believe in evil spirits?"

"They believe," Jim affirmed. "The Navajo are firmer in their traditional religious beliefs than most native people. But the Spirit Trail idea seems to come more from the traders than from the weavers."

Alexa wrinkled her brow. "What do you mean?"

"I know many weavers, including some who would

never dream of finishing a rug without a pathway, but they don't call it a Spirit Trail. They call it 'the weaver's pathway,' or 'my mind's road,' *shíni bittiin*. It's a way out of the pattern, all right, but for the weaver herself, not for any evil spirits.'' He paused. ''Has anyone talked to you about weaving sickness?''

''Yes,'' Kurt answered for her. ''We saw Dorothy Bighorse and her friends yesterday.''

''They call it 'being trapped in the rug' or 'trying to get out of the pattern,' '' Jim said. Alexa thought of her weaving dream again and shuddered. ''They believe that if they don't leave themselves a pathway out, their minds will become trapped in the pattern and they won't be able to make a new rug. I expect it comes from the Navajo fear of being enclosed. Even their hogans have a perpetually open door.''

''That's true,'' Alexa said, recalling the heavy rug that covered the open doorway at the Bighorse hogan. ''So where did the evil spirits come from?''

''Probably a mistranslation,'' Jim said. ''At least, that's my best guess. To a nonnative speaker of Navajo, shih-nee bih-teen sounds pretty much like chin-dee bih-teen.'' He emphasized the enunciation. ''I'd guess an early trader asked a weaver about the flaw in her rug, heard her use the word for evil spirits, *chi'íídii* or *chindi* instead of *shíní*, then stuck the label Spirit Trail on it and passed the idea around.''

Alexa shrugged. ''You have to admit it's a pretty compelling idea.''

Kurt nodded. ''Compelling, but not Navajo,'' he said. ''Right, bro?''

''Right. The idea of being trapped within your own pattern is much more like the people I know.'' He nodded toward their interview schedule, posted on the wall. "Just wait until you meet the weavers who use the pathway. You'll see what I mean."

"I'm looking forward to it," Alexa answered.

So am I, Kurt silently echoed as he followed Alexa to her car. His initial attraction had only grown since she had first arrived, and today— He paused on a long sigh. Today had been great. He'd never worked more easily with anyone, not even Meg. Alexa was a brilliant writer. He'd seen enough of her work by now to know. She was also a quick study. Already she knew as much about Navajo weaving as he did, or close enough, and she certainly asked the right questions. She was an invaluable addition to Rainbow Productions. If only she'd stay, she could be an invaluable addition to his life as well.

Aye, there's the rub, he quoted silently, vaguely wondering why his smattering of Shakespeare only showed up in moments of frustration. The day had been filled with magical moments, moments as mystical as McGee's evil spirits and ever so much lovelier. Alexa's face had been so alive, so full of passion. She loved what she was doing, and it showed all over her. There had been other moments too, more private moments, when he sensed that she was thinking of him, and the passion in her face had still been there.

Hence the frustration. There were those wonderful moments when it seemed they were made for each other and both of them knew it, but such moments were always followed by reminders of Burbank and the life Alexa planned elsewhere. Whenever Kurt pushed just a little, trying to find ways of encouraging her to stay, she got as skittish as a cornered kit fox.

What was it the Bard had said about how the course of true love never did run smooth?

"It's so good to have my own car back." Alexa smiled up at him from behind the wheel of her compact. "I guess I'll see you Monday, hmm?"

"Sooner than that," Kurt answered, trying to sound casual. "I've got some mail for the farm that was accidentally delivered to my place. I'll follow you out and turn it over to Mom."

Was he imagining it, or did Alexa's face fall when he said that? "Okay, then. I guess I'll see you in a few minutes."

"Right." He got in the pickup and followed her toward Rainbow Rock, then down the long lane to the farm, which put him in the perfect position to witness the scene when his brother Chris came out to greet her. He parked the truck and got out as quickly as possible, arriving just in time to see Chris offer Alexa a hand, then stand beside her, his arm possessively about her waist.

"Afternoon, bro," Chris drawled, clearly aware of Kurt's discomfiture—and enjoying it.

"Afternoon." In deference to the lady, Kurt kept his reply civil, if hardly loquacious. For a moment, no one spoke. Tension crackled in the air, as sharp as summer lightning.

"Something I can do for you?" Chris asked.

It occurred to Kurt that he'd been far too easy on Chris during their childhood. If he hadn't let him get away with so much then, maybe the grown-up Chris wouldn't be such a pain in the—

"Kurt has some mail for your mother," Alexa interjected helpfully.

Chris didn't move. "I believe Mom's in the kitchen."

"Thanks." Kurt didn't move either. Darned if he was going to let Chris get away with dismissing him like a nosy butler!

It was Alexa who broke the stalemate. "I'm looking forward to a tall glass of ice water myself, so I'm on my way to the kitchen. Let me take that for you." She reached for the letters and started for the house.

Kurt saw his moment. "I'll walk with you," he said, taking her elbow and glaring at Chris over his shoulder.

During the hour that followed, Kurt kept a close eye on his little brother, pressing the advantage whenever it arose. He even managed to wangle an invitation to stay to dinner, something he'd rarely done since declaring his independence and moving away. That resulted in another awkward meal with him on Alexa's left and Chris on her right, only this time Kurt kept up the running commentary, drawing Alexa out about Navajo rugs, weaving sickness, evil spirits, and the weaver's pathway. Remembering how Chris had monopolized her at dinner last Sunday, he made a point of touching her, also—light, friendly touches that he hoped would encourage rather than annoy her. *It seems to be working*, he thought as Alexa's sky-blue eyes lit up again.

Then the denouement. "Would you care to drive out and see the sunset with me tonight, Alexa?"

There was no question about it this time; her face fell like a stone. "I'm sorry, Kurt. I, uh, we . . . that is, Chris and I have plans this evening."

"Oh." So much for advantages. Feeling like he'd

just been kicked in the stomach, Kurt sifted his mind for an idea, anything to regain a little of the ground he'd just lost. "How about tomorrow? Maybe a picnic?"

"I'd like that," she answered brightly. It pleased him that she hadn't even looked at Chris before answering.

"Great. I'll pick you up about ten o'clock, okay?"

"Ten? Isn't that early for a picnic?"

"Not where we're going. Wear some good hiking shoes, okay?"

She smiled. It was one of those dazzling smiles that always left Kurt a little breathless. "Sounds great."

Then with a pointed look at his little brother, Kurt added, "We'll probably be gone all day—and into the evening."

My, but she had an expressive face! He could see the moment when that registered, and made her uncomfortable. "All day?"

"Don't worry. It'll be fun," he assured her.

Alexa seemed uneasy, but she covered well. "I'll see you in the morning then."

"Ten o'clock," he said, tipping his hat to her. As he drove away, a little faster than wisdom suggested, he couldn't help wondering where Chris planned to take her this evening, and what, if anything, he could do to break it up. Even more he wondered how he'd fill the day tomorrow with enough excitement to keep Alexa amused, but still at ease with him. Then he knew. "Grand Falls," he murmured aloud, and smiled in satisfaction.

* * *

"Kurt! It's spectacular!" Alexa stood at the edge of a precipice, staring down on one of the most stunning natural wonders she had ever seen.

"It is something, isn't it?"

"Amazing! And you say it isn't even on the map?"

"It isn't a regular feature," Kurt explained. "It's more a seasonal thing. This riverbed only runs full when there's heavy rain in the mountains." He pointed. "Over there. This week, with a warm rain on top of a heavy snowpack, it's running high."

Alexa followed the gesture. "It was raining there on Thursday," she said, almost yelling to be heard over the thundering waters, "when we were talking to the weavers."

"Right. Only we were on the other side of the mountains then."

They'd driven for nearly half a day just to reach this isolated spot, much of it on rain-gutted washboard roads or mere tire ruts. Kurt had stopped around noon, spreading a picnic blanket beneath a piñon pine and serving a light lunch of French bread and deli salads. Then they'd traveled on over roads that seemed to have no names and go nowhere. They were alone in the heart of the reservation.

And it was worth it. Alexa would happily travel twice the distance—at least, if she could travel with Kurt—to see what she was seeing now. A torrent of red-brown water beat against the sandy walls of the approaching wash, slowly eroding them in on itself, then plunged in fury into a canyon far below, blithely tossing giant logs like matchsticks. "How high do you think it is?" she asked, awed.

"Folks say it's higher than Niagara. I'd guess a good two hundred feet."

"Amazing," Alexa said again.

She'd had her doubts about this day, especially after the show Kurt and Chris had put on the evening before, both of them pricklier than porcupines and equally as friendly. It might have been flattering, if she hadn't felt so embarrassed for them both. Then there had been the evening with Chris—pleasant enough, light and fun, but this time she'd found herself missing the magic that lit the room whenever she was with Kurt. It was silly, especially since she planned to leave in less than a month, but she couldn't seem to resist. She never felt anything like it when she was with Chris, never with anyone else. Though wisdom suggested she should run from it, a small part of her wondered what would happen if she allowed herself, like the tides, to be drawn to his magnetic spell.

Her body responded before her mind did. Without realizing it, she moved closer to Kurt, brushing his shoulder. He smiled and slipped his arm around her, drawing her near.

"Amazing," she said for the third time, only this time she barely noticed the falls. Her eyes were riveted on Kurt's mouth. He seemed to be thinking the same thing. Slowly, as if drawn by a power beyond his control, he lowered his head. Slowly, responding to the same force, Alexa raised hers. Somewhere in the middle, their lips met.

It was magic. Alexa had almost decided she had exaggerated the effects of that first kiss. Surely nothing so simple could be so powerful, but she had been wrong. Like the simple water that raged with such dynamic power before them, this kiss was nothing less than spectacular. Kurt enveloped her, wrapping her in his arms and holding her so tightly against him that he almost crushed the breath out of her, and Alexa, freeing herself from the sling, clung just as tightly, hanging on like a drowning woman, molding herself to him and taking his breath for her own. It went on for a long time, drawing them into a vortex of passion and commitment, desire and promise, longing and fulfillment while the mist from the frenzied waters surrounded and enshrouded them, making them a part of the natural wonder.

Finally Kurt lifted his head, but still held her, one hand entangled in her hair, the other gently stroking her back. A couple of times, he started to speak, but didn't get far. If he felt as she did, Alexa reflected in wonder, he was probably unable to form cogent words. Finally he whispered, ''Wow.''

Wow indeed. Alexa was still reeling, her mind a kaleidoscope, her body a pillar of flame. She thought it a miracle that she hadn't already gone up in smoke.

''Alexa, are you all right?'' Kurt asked her after a moment.

''Umm,'' she answered, snuggling her head against his chest. They stood that way for a long time, feeling the beat of the waterfall, the beat of their blood. When Kurt finally suggested they should be on their way, Alexa responded sluggishly, bonelessly, struggling to force herself into simple steps.

Something irrevocable had happened there in the shadow of natural forces she couldn't quite comprehend. It was something she wanted and didn't want, desired and feared, and could never, ever change. As they began the long drive home, Alexa decided it was better if she simply didn't think about it. She had only four weeks left with Kurt McAllister and, knowing what she knew now, she planned to enjoy them all.

But this was still just a temporary stop on the way to her future. It would be well for her to remember that.

It's temporary, Kurt thought as they drove the rutted road away from Grand Falls. *It's only temporary. The lady is on her way to California, and you'd be wise to remember that.* The sun was beginning to set behind them, filling the sky with brilliant color and touching the high, spotty clouds with splashes of pink. *Temporary*, Kurt reminded himself sharply. Some small part of him couldn't help observing how very, very sad that was.

Chapter Six

Sunday was charmed. Alexa relished the McAllister family dinner, then read a nap-time story to Cassie, Joan's youngest, cuddling the towheaded toddler and enjoying it more than she'd remembered. At the weekly sing-along, she thrived on the attentions of not one but two handsome, blond McAllister men. It was odd, she reflected. Now that Kurt no longer seemed to feel the need to corner her attention, she enjoyed being around him much more. Whenever she looked up and caught him watching her, they exchanged small, tender smiles that brought back, for a moment, the magic that had surrounded them at Grand Falls. Later she guiltlessly enjoyed every bite of Kate's delicious peach cobbler, promising herself she'd hike it all off on the reservation.

She did too. On Monday she and Kurt visited the Shirleys, a family of four weavers near Pine Springs who taught them about natural herb dyes, then took them out tramping their own gardens and the surrounding desert to locate herbal sources. Alexa's legs soon ached as much as her writing hand.

She learned that a rich burgundy red came from the fruits of the prickly pear, while alder bark produced a bright true red; that imperial yellow came from wild holly root, while a softer shade was from yellow sweet clover; that the soft, mossy green preferred in Chinle blankets actually came from moss—the green lichen that grew on wood, while dark, rich green derived, surprisingly, from red onion skin. Brown onion skin yielded a soft orange, while bright-green Brigham tea produced a muted mustard yellow. In all, she catalogued more than sixty natural vegetable dyes from the deepest black (sumac or piñon pitch) to the brightest red (cochineal, an insect) to the softest blue-gray and mauve, made from juniper mistletoe and globemallow. Priscilla Shirley told her more than two hundred fifty natural dyes were known to native weavers.

Later, after a lunch of beans and frybread in their hogan, the women of the Shirley family showed Kurt and Alexa how to mix dye. Each dye required a mordant, a fixative such as alum, baking soda, or juniper ash. Agnes Shirley explained, while Kurt translated, that the final color depended on a half-dozen variables including the plant type or species, the season harvested and the region of the harvest, which parts of the plant were used and in what concentration, how long the wool stayed in the dye bath, the mixture of dye types, and whether they used fresh or dried plant material.

Alexa learned that most dyes were prepared hot,

even boiling, and that weavers often kept a variety of large cast-iron kettles just for that purpose. She watched in fascination as the Shirley women split wood, built a fire, drew water from a shallow well, and filled two large cast-iron kettles, then put them on to boil. When the water reached a full boil, the women brought out the dried leaves and blossoms of the feathery cassia plant, and mixed two pounds of cassia (measured on a small kitchen scale) with a quarter cup of raw alum into each pot. As the pots boiled again, the yarn was added, one pound to each. For the next hour, the women took turns supervising and stirring the boiling pots with long sticks until Ruby Shirley decided the color was right. Using their poles, they drew the yarn from the boiling pots and hung it from a low-lying limb of the sycamore tree beside their hogan. The result was two pounds of yellow-green yarn.

As Kurt drove her home that evening, Alexa commented on the labor-intensive nature of the craft, and Kurt answered that even at the prices some rugs now commanded, a weaver often earned less than two dollars an hour. As he walked her to the door, the magic sparkled between them briefly, but Chris managed to quash it by opening the door to greet Alexa. Kurt bit his lip, aware that Chris' work on the farm gave him the distinct advantage, but he smiled as he told her he'd pick her up in the morning. At least when they were traveling, he had Alexa to himself.

Tuesday took them to Flagstaff, where a history professor at Northern Arizona University taught them about the Long Walk and Bosque Redondo, the forced removal of the Navajos from their beloved *Dinehtah* to harsh imprisonment in an arid, isolated region of eastern New Mexico. "Kit Carson was charged with the removal," Professor Robbins explained for Kurt's camera. "He didn't have the firepower to force so many Indians, so he starved them out. Over a period of about three years, he methodically burned their fields, groves, and hogans and slaughtered their herds. By 1864, most Navajos were relocated."

As he talked, Alexa felt growing sorrow for the deprivation of those early people. "At least they could be fed there," she said over the lump in her throat.

"Not really," Robbins answered. "The federal government, still fighting the Civil War in the east, wasn't prepared to feed so many starving people. Conditions in the camp were deplorable, but still expensive to maintain. It wasn't long before the public outcry was not to round up 'wild' Navajos, but to let the others go. In 1868 the government did."

"Back to their own homeland?" Alexa asked. When Robbins answered yes, she responded, "Thank goodness!"

"But they could never go back to the way things had been," he continued. "Their styles of dress and weaving, for instance, had changed forever. Before the Long Walk, the Navajos owned nearly a quarter of a million sheep, and they dressed entirely in cloth of their own making. They left Bosque Redondo with fewer than a thousand sheep. During the four years of imprisonment, they learned to make clothing from the cotton trade cloth the government gave them in styles worn by the Anglos there. What was in style for Anglo women in the 1860s is what Navajo women still wear."

"I remember," Alexa answered, thinking of the ankle-length satin or calico skirts and velvet "prairie blouses" worn by all the Navajo women she'd met. "I only thought of the style as Navajo. Now I realize it must have been what the wives of mid-1860s army officers wore."

"Exactly," Robbins answered. He went on to talk about the revival of weaving on the reservation lands. Alexa learned that the government had eventually made good on its promise to restore fifteen thousand sheep to the Indians, but the sheep they sent were merinos, not the Spanish *churros* the Navajos had once raised. The wool was different, greasier and with shorter fibers, and native weavers had difficulty working it. In Robbins' opinion, traders like Hubbell and "Cozy" McSparron and collectors like Mary Cabot Wheelwright had kept the craft alive. "They helped the weavers through the transition, arranging to have the wool professionally cleaned and carded, hunting up old recipes for vegetal dyes, finding weavers who could teach the craft to the young. Had it not been for their efforts, traditional weaving might have died."

"Fascinating, isn't it?" Alexa asked Kurt later as they drove away from the campus. "It was the larger Anglo culture that devastated Navajo life, and it was Anglos who helped them reestablish some of the old ways."

"I guess in the long run, most folks work from self-interest," Kurt observed. "It was the settlers' fear of Navajo raiders that forced the removal, it was concern for taxpayer dollars that caused the outcry against the encampment at Bosque Redondo, and it was profit motive that encouraged the traders to revive native crafts."

"I suppose that's true," Alexa said, not really wanting to believe it, "but I hate to think it was all self-interest. Don't you think there were some who tried to help the Indians rebuild for altruistic reasons?"

"You mean, out of the goodness of their hearts?"

"Well, yes."

Kurt shrugged. "Maybe so, maybe not. There were wonderful people like Father Berard, who spent his life studying Navajo language and culture to create the first written alphabet, but was he motivated by altruism, or by his desire to win the approval of the church?"

Alexa raised a brow. "Feeling a bit cynical, are we?"

He grinned. "Not really." He paused at a stoplight just before the freeway entrance, and leisurely took a lock of her hair into his fingers. "There's nothing wrong with a little healthy self-interest, especially when what one person wants is good for everyone involved."

The air around them suddenly snapped with electricity, as Alexa realized they were no longer talking about Navajo history. Her face warmed and she lowered her eyes, unable to meet the intensity she saw in Kurt's. Then the light changed and the moment passed. They were soon on the freeway and on their way home again. Talk of Navajo weaving and their progress on the project absorbed them as they headed east.

They had worked late on the university campus and darkness had fallen before they got to Winslow, so Kurt suggested they stop for dinner at a Mexican café he knew. Alexa ordered a marvelous turkey tamale with red chili sauce and found that she laughed often during their meal, amused by Kurt's stories of growing up on the McAllister farm. She also found she could talk easily of what it had been like to grow up on the Babbidge farm in Henderson, Kentucky, just south of the Indiana border. Few of the friends she had met at Columbia could appreciate the humor involved in burying a little brother up to his neck in the corncrib, or releasing an albino peacock to spread its tail and shriek on the porch of the neighborhood drunk, just after the bars closed.

Kurt appreciated, and laughed along with her. As they walked away from the restaurant to the truck again, she cast him several sideways glances. Why'd he have to be so nice? she wondered. It would have been easier to drive away if he'd been a self-involved egomaniac, or a jerk.

He opened her door for her, then got in on the driver's side, but he didn't start the truck immediately. "Alexa," he said, as if he'd been pondering it for a while, "I'm really enjoying working with you."

Alexa waited. Since he said nothing more, she said, "I'm enjoying working with you too, Kurt."

Then he turned and moved toward her, his eyes twinkling. "I really enjoyed kissing you last weekend too."

She grinned. "You know I did too."

With mock seriousness, he continued. "I think I'd enjoy kissing you again, but if I wait till we get to the porch, Chris will be there."

Alexa couldn't help it; she giggled. "I expect you're right," she agreed, trying to keep a straight face.

"So what if I were to kiss you good night right

here? Then I could drive you home after. What do you think?''

''I thought you'd never ask,'' she said, and slipped into his arms.

Could lightning strike three times in the same place? A full two minutes later, Alexa had decided it could. She never knew whether he had prompted her to let him deepen the kiss, or whether she had opened her lips to invite him; whether he had pushed them away from the steering column or she had drawn him to her; whether it was his heartbeat that echoed so resoundingly in her ears or her own. What she knew was that she could live a lifetime for such kisses.

When it finally ended, they replayed the moments after their kiss by the falls—holding each other, Kurt stroking her hair and feathering it with light kisses, touching her back and arms with gentling strokes, both of them too overcome to speak.

''That seemed like a good idea at the time.'' Kurt finally spoke, his voice a husky whisper. ''Now I'm not sure I'm going to be fit to drive.''

''Don't look at me,'' she whispered back. ''My bones are mush.''

He sighed. ''My word, Alexa, but you are something.''

''Look who's talking!''

He smiled, but his eyes were suddenly serious. ''You know this kind of magic doesn't happen every day.''

''I know,'' she said, then pulled away, straightening her clothing. ''And now I think it's time to go home.''

''Alexa . . .''

''Kurt, please don't say anything. Not now.''

He paused, as if fighting his instincts. "All right, but we're going to have to talk about it sometime."

Alexa shrugged noncommittally, hoping that some-time simply wouldn't come. Forty-five minutes later, when Kurt walked her to the door at his mother's house, Chris stepped out to greet them, and they chuckled at the shared joke. "What's so funny?" Chris asked, sending them both into new peals of laughter.

"I'll see you in the morning," she said to Kurt, squeezing his hand before she pushed past Chris and up the stairs to her, to Kurt's, room. Even as she went, she knew he was right. They were going to have to talk about it—sometime.

On Wednesday, near Klagetoh, weaver Annie Tso-sie demonstrated how patterns were created. Kurt kept his camera focused on Annie as she taught Alexa how to form a "shed" by passing a long, flat stick, called a shed rod, behind alternate warp threads. This held every other warp forward and created an opening, a shed, for the passage of a weft. Then Annie turned her tools over to Alexa and invited her to place a weft strand into the shed she had created, adding to a black interior pattern she was developing in the rug.

Kurt knew they couldn't use the footage of Alexa weaving in their documentary, but still he kept the Betacam running. There she sat, her trim figure framed by the loom, her silver-blond hair coaxed by the breeze, her face alight with marvelous energy. She laughed as Annie urged her fingers onto the tools and into the rug, then showed her how to use a fork-shaped tool to tamp the thread as she placed it. Kurt felt his heart constrict with a tender longing he didn't dare name, and kept taping. If he couldn't persuade her to talk about what was happening between them, if he couldn't lure her into giving them a chance, then in less than a month she'd be on her way to fame and stardom in California, and these lovely images would be all he would have of her.

Later Annie taught Alexa how to use the heddle rod to reverse the shed, moving the back-lying warps forward, and how to weave large portions of a pattern in one place before moving into a different position in front of the loom. Kurt dutifully taped it all, changing the camera position from time to time to get a better angle, or to take best advantage of the ambient light, but already he knew which of the day's tapes he liked best, and which he would keep long after the documentary was done.

On their way home that evening, he decided he'd better corner Alexa's plans for the weekend before his brother had the chance. "Have you made any plans for Saturday?" he asked. "I thought we might see some sights."

"Anything like Grand Falls?" she asked.

"Sorry. That's a one-of-a-kind show. There are other things, though."

"I'd love to, but I'm afraid I do have plans. Chris asked me to go out in the dune buggy with him on Saturday."

Kurt felt a momentary rush of frustration, then a light went on. He grinned. "Do you suppose he'd mind if I invited myself along?"

Alexa chuckled, a sound like the March wind sighing through the cottonwoods. "I'm sure he would."

"Then consider me invited. What time shall I be there?"

Alexa smiled and shook her head. "You're really something, you know that? He said we'd leave around mid-morning."

"I'll be there at first light." He gave her knee a possessive squeeze.

She took his hand and put it back on the wheel. "You know, attention like this could turn a woman's head."

"I keep hoping." Alexa laughed again, and again Kurt felt the warm constriction around his heart.

Thursday took them to talk with another weaver, one who specialized in Yei rugs and sand-painting designs. It was a frustrating day, the roads soggy with snow runoff and barely passable. Then the weaver refused to discuss the holy patterns, beyond saying that the rugs spoke for themselves. Fortunately she did show them several excellent examples which would make good visuals to put behind the voices in the Robbins and McGee interviews when they edited the final program. She also took a moment to point out the Rainbow Goddess, the beautiful squared-U arch that surrounded her sand-painting pattern on three sides. Kurt figured that gave them about eight seconds of usable tape, not much for the kind of day they'd spent.

They worked together in the office on Friday, cataloging the work they had already done and catching Meg up on what they'd accomplished while Cretia kept the office running. Though Meg claimed to be feeling well and complained about having to stay down "while you folks are having all the fun," by mid-afternoon she was having contractions again, and Kurt volunteered to take her home.

"Don't forget dinner tonight," Meg said to Alexa as she gathered her things and pulled on her rain slicker. "You and Kurt, seven o'clock."

"Sure you're up to it?" Alexa asked. "We could wait until you're feeling better, or maybe we can bring the dinner."

"I'd be happy to help," Kurt volunteered.

"Actually, Jim's doing the cooking, so it's no trouble for me," Meg assured her. "It'll be simple, just pasta and a salad, but it'll be a chance for us to get acquainted, and I can catch up on what's going on with the project while I'm sitting around with my feet up."

Kurt looked to Alexa and nodded. "Then I'll look forward to it," Alexa said. Kurt waved to her and Cretia as he went out the door into a light rain.

Thirty minutes later when he pulled up in the alley behind the office, a mucky puddle had formed around the back door. Choosing to keep his boots dry, he used the storeroom door instead. He was just about to enter the office, his hand on the partially open door, when he heard Alexa say his name. Feeling like a sneak and a fool, he leaned close to the door and listened.

"He's been so good to me," Alexa was saying. "No damsel in distress should be without a rescuer like him."

"He's been mighty good to me too, especially after the way I acted. And by the way, you two certainly had an interesting start to your relationship."

"There's really no relationsh—"

"Yeah, I knew you'd say that." Cretia's voice rang

with a teasing lilt, then grew wistful. "Danny and I started off well too. He always seemed so gallant, so much in charge, and it was easy for me to just glide along and let him take care of everything."

"Big mistake, huh?" Alexa prompted.

"*Big* mistake. By the time things got rough, I felt trapped. I had no education, no job skills, I'd never worked . . . Heck, I didn't even know how to balance a checkbook. Danny always took care of that."

Kurt leaned so he could see. He watched Alexa reach out to pat Cretia's arm. "Don't feel alone. That's apparently a pretty typical pattern."

Cretia leaned forward. "How'd you get so wise? Was your parents' marriage bad?"

"My parents? Heavens, no! They're like a romantic sitcom, even after twenty-eight years, though their story could have been like yours, I suppose. They married right out of high school and Daddy went to work farming his father's land until Papaw died and turned the place over to him." Alexa's voice grew sad. "I always wondered if Mama didn't regret having so many of us so quickly, and being poor all the time. I worried that she might have had dreams of her own that got buried under diapers and laundry."

"Is that why you're so leary of commitments?"

Kurt almost choked on the bald question. He'd known Cretia could be bold, but he wouldn't have dared to ask Alexa something so personal. He saw Alexa shrug.

"You noticed, huh?"

"Honey, we've *all* noticed. Is it just the lure of Hollywood, or is there something more to your skittishness?"

Alexa sighed. "You know, I probably shouldn't answer that question."

Cretia shrugged. "Up to you, but if you want to talk, your secret is safe with me. I've learned the hard way what happens when everybody thinks they have the right to judge your life."

Kurt heard her promise of confidentiality and felt even guiltier about listening in, just not quite guilty enough to back away from the door—at least, not until he heard Alexa's answer.

She took a deep breath. "The lure of Hollywood is a big part of it. I learned as a kid to hate being poor." She leaned back in her chair and took a second breath. "Because of the farm, we always had plenty to eat, and we kids got along well, so we never worried about entertainment, but people were always giving us their old clothes and I got teased about my hand-me-down dresses. I never had more than one pair of shoes at a time until I was old enough to work and buy my own. I never owned socks of my own, either, until I went away to Columbia. Mine always came out of the family sock box."

"Whew!" Cretia rocked her chair back. "I thought my kids were having it rough!"

"It probably wasn't as bad as I'm making it sound," Alexa demurred, "but I've got to tell you that the idea of a contract with a major studio looks to me like the pot of gold at the rainbow's end. I could buy a home of my own, wear new clothes whenever I felt like shopping, indulge a little. I could even do some nice things for my family. You know, see that the younger ones get to go to college, put a new roof on the house, get Mama a microwave. . . ."

"You don't have to do it all yourself, you know. If you marry a man who has money—"

"I can end up just like you did, or like my Aunt Bobbie." Alexa paused. "I'm sorry, Cretia. I shouldn't have said that."

Cretia patted her hand. "It's okay. It's true, but now you do have to tell me about Aunt Bobbie."

Alexa sighed. "You know the story. She married young, depended on her husband to take care of her, then found out he was a creep. She left him five or six times before it finally took. He just kept promising her he'd changed. By then, she had a couple of little kids and needed his income, so she just kept going back. Finally we had to take them in. By then there were four children, and the cramped conditions made things pretty difficult for all of us, but it was the only way Bobbie had a chance. When I saw that, I swore I'd never be dependent on anyone to support me or my kids."

"With the kind of skills you have, you'll always be able to get work if you need to, Alexa."

"I suppose so, but it's more than that. Writing is what I've wanted to do my whole life, and getting onto a show like 'Mountain Magic' is like playing in the major leagues. It's my chance to prove that I can play hardball with the big boys."

"It really means a lot to you, doesn't it?" Cretia asked, speaking the words that had just formed in Kurt's mind.

"You can't imagine how much," Alexa answered.

Kurt backed away from the office door. The warm constriction around his heart now felt like a tight fist trying to wring the life out of him. His mother had always told him that people who eavesdropped heard bad news about themselves. *Maybe I should have listened to Mom*, he thought as he quietly slipped into the alleyway, then came back in, wet boots and all, through the regular door.

"The manicotti is delicious, isn't it, Kurt?" Alexa asked. She'd been charmed by Jim and Meg's beautiful cliffside home, lured by the savory pasta dish and fresh, crisp salad, but her dinner companion had been distant, almost unreachable. In fact, he'd seemed preoccupied much of the afternoon.

"Yes, delicious," Kurt said, returning to them.

Though the conversation went on, and Kurt seemed to be holding up his end, Alexa promised herself to keep an eye on him. If something was bothering Kurt, and if it was anything she could help, she certainly owed it to him to try.

Meg asked for more details about their travels and interviews during the week and they both pitched in, filling in stories about the Yei weaver who wouldn't talk and the university professor who wouldn't stop talking. After a time, Meg suggested Alexa might like to have a tour of the house. "Maybe you can show Kurt and Alexa around, dear, while I sit here with my feet up," she said to Jim. "You know, I so seldom get a chance to do that anymore."

"Sarcasm becomes you, sweetheart," Jim said, kissing his wife. Then, "Come on, you two. Let me show you what we've done with the nursery."

As they moved from room to room, listening to Jim's cursory monologue, Alexa saw much of what she'd always dreamed of in a home of her own. It was secure and airy, spacious and still cozy, formal enough for entertaining, yet inviting and homey. She was able to identify the rugs she saw on the floors—a Ganado, a Burntwater, a storm pattern, two fine *yeibichai* wall tapestries—then when she spotted and identified a pathway in one beautifully bordered Two Gray Hills rug, Jim showed her a similar border on a Navajo basket he kept in a glass cabinet. That border was also broken, the artist having left a clear pathway out of the pattern.

"You see what I mean?" he said. "The Navajos always want a way out."

Like me, Alexa thought, remembering her conversation with Lucretia that afternoon. When she looked up, Kurt was staring at her so intently, she'd have sworn he'd read her mind.

Jim led them down the hall to the nursery where he showed them a confection of a room in white eyelet with yellow trim.

"I take it you don't know yet whether it's a girl or a boy," Alexa asked.

"The doctor might know, but we asked him not to tell us," Jim answered. "We want to be surprised."

"And I'm sure you'll be happy with whatever you get," she said.

"Of course," he answered, and Alexa knew he meant it.

Later that evening when Kurt finally drove her home, they had the coming baby to talk about as well as their project, but Kurt still seemed as remote as central Asia. Alexa, who'd been hoping for another of those mind-blowing kisses, felt distinctly disappointed when he walked her to the door, greeted Chris as he came out to meet them, then left, not even mentioning the plans they'd made for him to join the dune buggy ride on Saturday. As he drove away, she wondered if she'd said or done something to hurt him. For the life of her, she couldn't think what it might be, but if there was anything—well, anything reasonable—that she could do, she'd move heaven and earth to do it. She owed him so much already.

Chapter Seven

"Will you please be more careful?" Kurt snapped at Chris for the fifth time in an hour.

"What's with you, bro? You getting old on me or something?" Chris gunned the dune buggy over another hill, catching some air on the resulting drop. "Wow! This is something, huh?"

The last question was clearly directed at Alexa. Her face flushed with exhilaration, she heartily agreed. Kurt felt like growling. Crashing this party had seemed like a good idea when he'd suggested it last week, but since he'd overheard Alexa talking with Cretia yesterday, he'd wondered whether he shouldn't just cut his losses before he allowed himself to get in any deeper. Now that he was out here, watching Chris and Alexa together and seeing how much fun she was having, well—

"Something wrong, bro? You look like somebody sat on your pet cat."

Kurt bared his teeth in what he hoped looked like a grin. If it wasn't convincing to begin with, it certainly didn't look any better when Chris took them over a bone-shattering series of ups and downs known locally as "the elevator hills."

"Let's run up the wash ways," Chris shouted above the noise of the engine, revving the little buggy over the rim of the arroyo that dropped ten or twelve feet into the dry riverbed.

Kurt hung on tightly to the backseat grips. "Bad idea, Chris. There was a warm rain in the mountains this morning. Given how much snow there was still standing up there last week, I think—"

"I think you sound like an old woman," Chris challenged. "Come on! Live a little! Have some fun."

Kurt thought of Grand Falls running high. "Chris, I really don't think it's a good idea," he repeated. "You've lived in the desert your whole life. You know better than to hang out in low places during the runoff."

"It's not like we're gonna *stay* here," Chris said, his voice clearly carrying a challenge.

Kurt looked to Alexa for some support and saw instead a pleading look. She sat in the front next to Chris, her whole face asking him to please relax and stop ruining the party. Despite the sling on her arm, she was having the time of her life. He shut up, wondering if Chris might be right about the old woman part. He was beginning to sound like a real party pooper.

Half a mile or so up the arroyo, Chris pulled the

dune buggy to a stop in a flurry of mud and sand. "There's a cool rock formation just over that ridge, Alexa. It's no Grand Falls, but I bet you'll like it. Come on!" he said, unbuckling his safety belt. "Go on ahead. We'll be right with you," Kurt said sternly.

Chris smiled knowingly. "All right, bro. But just to make sure you don't take off without me . . ." He winked at Kurt as he dropped the ignition keys into his pocket, and struck out for the wall of the wash.

As he climbed out of sight, Kurt turned to Alexa. "How's your arm? I notice you're still wearing the sling." Even as he spoke, he knew he was fussing again. Why couldn't he just relax and stop worrying?

"It's okay," she answered. "Pretty tender up here where the break is, but it's better now."

"Just as long as you're okay," Kurt answered awkwardly.

Then he heard it. At first, he thought it was thunder rumbling distantly in the hills, but instead of going away, it grew louder. And he knew. *Please don't let this be happening,* he prayed silently, and began ripping off his belt. "Alexa, get clear. Hurry. *Hurry!*"

"What on earth?" she asked. "Kurt, what's going on?"

"Flash flood!" he screamed. "Get your belt off. Get clear! *Hurry!*"

Alexa paled, then popped the seat belt and started pulling it over her head, but the sling kept getting in her way. Before she could finish, Kurt was free and was helping her out of her belt, then he was out of the buggy on the earth beside her, yanking her out of the cab.

"Run!" he shouted. "Make for the wall of the

wash, the way Chris went.'' Alexa began to run, then groaned in pain and cradled the sling at her side. ''Run!'' Kurt yelled again, grabbing her free hand and dragging her through the wet sand.

Alexa tripped and went down with a thud that knocked the breath out of her. Cursing under his breath, Kurt picked her up like a flour sack, threw her over his shoulder, and ran for the wall. As he started climbing, he could hear Alexa choking back sobs of fear and pain. Then he saw the water.

Rounding the curve in the wash less than a hundred feet away, the wall of brown froth rushed at them, four to five feet high and driving forward with phenomenal power and speed. Using all the energy he could summon, Kurt hurled Alexa forward and upward, wishing he could take the time to be more gentle with her. She hit with another thud and a moan, but rolled out of the way, making space for him to follow.

He scrambled, but the water hit him before he was quite to the top, catching at his legs below the knees, and loosening his grip on the rocks near the rim.

''Kurt!'' Alexa screamed, reaching for him.

He grabbed her hand, then the rock, and gave one huge pull, dragging himself free of the flood. He flopped down beside Alexa just in time to see the water hit the dune buggy, roll it under, and carry it away as easily as if it were a child's toy.

Chris came running up behind them. ''What the—''

''Flash flood.'' Kurt cut him off.

''Holy—'' Chris ran one hand through his hair in a gesture of abject frustration, watching as the dune buggy disappeared in the wash that was suddenly a tumultuous river. "Kurt, I'm so sorry. I never thought—"

"I know you didn't," Kurt said more gently than he wanted, then he turned his back on his little brother and carefully took Alexa into his arms. "Are you all right? Did I hurt you?"

She was crying. "Oh, no, Kurt. You saved my life." Her face was starkly white, her blue eyes enormous, her tears running freely. She held her left arm against her, but used her right hand to stroke his face. "Kurt, you saved my life."

"Thank goodness," he said. "I'm so sorry, Alexa. I didn't want to hurt you. If anything had happened to you . . ." He stopped, too choked with emotion to continue.

Kurt and Alexa sat on the bank of the raging river, tenderly holding each other, murmuring comforting words, stroking with gentle touches, rocking in a soothing rhythm. Behind them, Chris looked from one to the other and slowly smiled.

The walk home had been less strenuous than Kurt had feared. Luckily they were on the right side of the wash and didn't have to find a way to cross it. Then Chris, feeling penitent, had run most of the way home, gotten his pickup truck, and come back to meet Kurt and Alexa halfway. Alexa was pale from shock and in pain, but she was a trouper. She had done what needed to be done and had done it without complaint. Nor had she blamed Kurt for the pain he had caused her. She had walked at his side, making an effort to keep up the pace and thanking him repeatedly for getting her out of harm's way. "That's twice now that you've rescued me," she had said as they neared the farm-house. "You know I can never repay you."

"If I'd had more sense to begin with, you never would have been in that situation," he'd answered, "and you don't need to repay anything. You pulled me out at the crucial moment too, remember?"

She was upstairs now, soaking in a hot bath. His mother had taken over as soon as the truck pulled up, wrapping Alexa in a blanket and shepherding her up the stairs to where a hot herbal bath had already been run. Kurt sat by the fireplace, warming himself with a cup of hot tea.

"Hey, bro. Can we talk?"

Kurt looked up as Chris entered the room. He set the cup down. "Sure, Chris, but there's really not much to—"

"I owe you an apology, a *big* apology."

Kurt shrugged. "You already said you were sorry, and I know you didn't realize how dangerous that wash was or you would never have taken the buggy down there."

"That's true, but it was a stupid thing to do, any-way—stupid and irresponsible. I just want you to know I'm sorry."

"You were showing off," Kurt said, but it was less an accusation than an observation.

"You're right, I was." He grinned and his eyes twinkled wickedly. "Can you blame me?"

Darned if Chris didn't have a winning smile. He'd always been able to get Kurt to forgive him anything, even when they were little kids. Kurt relaxed. "No, I don't blame you."

"But that's not the only apology I owe you," Chris

went on, squatting in front of his brother's chair so the two were eye-to-eye. "I've been giving you a run for your money with Alexa. It seemed like a fun game."

Kurt dropped his eyes, unwilling to let his brother see what he might find there. "You're certainly right about that one," he said, sipping the tea to control his voice. "You've surely been giving me a run for my money."

"But it isn't a game with you, is it?"

Kurt swallowed hard and met Chris's eyes. They were dead serious. So were his own. "No, it isn't a game."

"Brother dear, are you in love with Alexa?" Chris asked.

There was no evading the sincerity in his brother's expression, and there was no denying the answer that rose immediately in his heart. Alexa was the puzzle piece, the one important thing that had been missing from his life. "I'm afraid I am."

Chris blinked. "That's a problem?"

"She doesn't want me, Chris. She doesn't want small-town life at all. She's wary of men, afraid to make a commitment, and almost pathological about being poor. To her, that screenwriter's job in Hollywood is the pot of gold at the end of the rainbow." Kurt realized his eyes were growing misty. "In about three weeks, she's going to get in that ugly little car of hers and drive away from me, and there's not a single thing I can do about it."

Chris rocked back on his heels. "Whew! That *is* a problem."

"So you see," Kurt continued, "competition with

my little brother was the least of my worries.'' He punctuated the comment with a wry grin.

Chris socked him in the shoulder, a brotherly gesture. ''Couldn't resist that, could you?'' Then he sobered. ''Look, bro. You have my blessing. Not that you need it—I don't think your lady was ever very interested in me, but I'm bowing out. And if there's anything I can do to plead your case, or to make it tougher for her to leave, you just say the word. I'm at your service.''

Kurt clapped his arms around his brother and thumped him a time or two, then drew back. ''If I can think of anything, you'll be the first to hear.''

''I could blow up her car,'' Chris offered facetiously.

Kurt tightened his mouth in a smirk. ''You're going to have trouble enough trying to find your own.''

''True,'' Chris answered, though he didn't have the grace to look worried. ''That wash empties into the Little Colorado right above the diversion dam. I figure the buggy will lodge around there someplace. I'll take the pickup out after the water goes down and drive till I find it. Fixing it up will give me something to do in the evenings—now that I'm not going to be busy with Alexa.''

Kurt smiled and Chris stood. ''Oh, and one more thing.''

''What's that?'' Kurt answered.

''When you two have a boy, will you name him after me?''

Kurt picked up the magazine from the table beside him and threw it at his brother's head. ''Get out of here, you idiot,'' he groused. Chris dodged, then darted away laughing.

For Alexa, the next days passed in a blur of happy activity. She enjoyed church and the McAllister family Sunday even more this week, now that she knew everyone better. Then with Monday morning, she and Kurt were traveling again, this time to Santa Fe to tape valuable footage at the Maxwell Museum of Anthropology on the University of New Mexico campus, and to talk with historians there. It was a two-day visit, with an overnight at a small but nicely appointed hotel. Kurt was the perfect host, perfect coworker, perfect gentleman. When he kissed her good night at her door, Alexa felt the threads of their lives joining more closely, being woven together in an intimate tapestry.

She came away from the museum with renewed appreciation for the man Kurt McAllister was, along with a raft of new knowledge about the classic period, chiefs' blankets, revival dyes, and the history of Navajo textiles. As they drove home Tuesday evening, she sat beside Kurt, reviewing her notes. ''The general belief is that the Navajo learned weaving from the Pueblo people, the people they called the Kisani, correct?''

''That's the way I heard it,'' Kurt affirmed.

''Then why is it that the Navajos still weave so well and the craft is nearly gone among the Pueblo people?''

''Hard to say,'' Kurt answered. ''Professor Robbins believes the Pueblo tribes were busy with so many other crafts, such as pottery making and silversmithing, that they dropped the emphasis on weaving after trade cloth became available. In the meantime, the Navajos had been buying their ceramics from the Pueblo tribes around them and making weaving an art form. The Navajos maintained weaving when the Pueblos lost it because it was more important to them.''

''Makes sense,'' Alexa agreed, adding the idea to her notes.

''But there are still other cultures that weave,'' Kurt continued. ''Our documentary is specifically about the Navajo craft, but if we were looking at native weaving in general, you'd be surprised what we could find.''

''Like what?''

''Like the Chilkat blankets of the Tlingit people, for instance.''

''I've seen pictures of those,'' Alexa said. ''Very elaborate, lots of black and white and yellow.''

''Right, and shaped to drape over a person's shoulders. They're often used ceremonially.''

''What else?'' Alexa asked, putting her notes down.

''Weaving is still practiced among the Hopi too,'' Kurt said. ''In their culture, it's almost exclusively done by men.''

''No kidding!'' Alexa forgot all about her notes. ''Do they still weave for everyday use, or mostly for ceremonial purposes?''

''They're like most people. What they can buy in town is good enough for everyday, but they can still put hundreds of hours into preparing something special.''

''For example?''

''For example, a bride's trousseau. The old custom among the Hopis was for a prospective bridegroom to weave the ceremonial wedding clothing for his intended before he proposed marriage. If she accepted, he offered her a full trousseau made by his own hands. The work was considered proof of his devotion as well as evidence of his ability to provide for a wife. Nowadays the young men are often employed in the outside world, but the tradition continues with the actual weaving done by older members of the groom's family.''

''That's fascinating.'' Alexa pondered briefly. ''What's in a bridal trousseau for a Hopi? I mean, is the clothing like the woolen blankets that we've been studying?''

''There's some wool, but the Hopi work largely in cotton. A bridal trousseau usually begins with a plain black wool dress and sometimes a brightly colored belt. It's always topped off with a unique white handwoven cotton sash that represents the groom's imagination and skill. He gives that to her carefully protected in a reed mat.''

''Fascinating,'' Alexa said again.

''But the most important part of the trousseau is the two plain white cotton *mantas* that go with it.''

''*Mantas?*''

''That's the Spanish word for a cloak or shawl. When a Hopi bride marries, she wears two large blanket-shaped shawls draped over her. Both of them are in spotless white, one slightly larger than the other. The smaller one will become highly useful after the wedding, since she can cut it up to serve many purposes in her new home, sometimes even to be the swaddling clothes for her first baby.''

''That's a nice thought,'' Alexa said. ''And the larger shawl?''

"The larger one is worn only once, at her wedding. After that it is carefully wrapped and preserved to be used again only once, as her burial shroud."

Alexa felt a chill. "Her *shroud?* Isn't that rather . . . gruesome?"

"Not when you think as the Hopis do." Kurt smiled gently. "When a Hopi lover offers his intended her trousseau, he is promising to love and cherish her for the rest of her life—and even beyond. When she marries him, she knows she'll go to her last rest wrapped in the gift of his love."

Alexa blinked. "I hadn't thought of it that way. It's . . . tender." What she didn't mention was the sense of mixed warmth and suffocation that swept over her as she realized the commitment involved in a Hopi marriage. A woman who accepted her wedding gown and her shroud from the same man was *serious* about spending her life with him.

Kurt reached across and squeezed her hand. "There are many native traditions we would do well to keep," he said, and again Alexa wondered if he was reading her mind.

Later, when he walked her to his mother's door, she saw Chris inside and smiled, sure the younger brother would interrupt them, but Chris grinned and went up the stairs while Kurt pushed his Stetson back and took a long, slow time to say good night. She wasn't sure what had passed between the two brothers since last Saturday, but she liked it—very much.

Wednesday took them on another two-day excursion, this time to the west. They started at a hogan near Tuba City, where Rosie Nakai had gathered several weavers from her family to talk about the pathway. Alexa took notes while Kurt kept the camera rolling, but the women seemed more interested in working out the concept for themselves than in clarifying it for them.

"That's why you make the pathway," a second woman said. "If you put the one yarn all the way through, then your brain can think forward."

"*Adaage de tlo* means you close yourself in," a cousin clarified. "It means you close your mind in."

"Some people think they might weave themselves in the rug and they put that line in so they can get out," another said.

Another weaver answered, "That's right. You close yourself in the weaving. You weave yourself in and there is no way out of the design."

"*Adaa* means 'path through,'" the cousin said again. "*Adaage de tlo* means you don't make a path through. You weave over the path of yourself."

"It's for the design," the fifth woman said. "It's a gateway to let the design out so you can use it again. It's my way of saying, 'Thank you for letting me use this design, and I'd like to use it again sometime.'"

"When I put it in, I think to myself, 'This is so my next rug can be even better,'" Rosie said.

The women went on for some time, but there was no talk of evil spirits or devils and Alexa realized Jim had probably been right in his assessment of the misnamed Spirit Trail. When the conversation began to wind down, she asked about the idea of the *chindi bitiin*.

"No, no." One woman spoke urgently as the others all shook their heads. "The Pathway is for the weaver. It's her Path. You know what *chindi* are. Well, *bitiin* means 'it's their trail,' like a trail for the *chindi*. But that's not what a Pathway is. The two things are different.''

"My mother and aunties taught me to weave," the younger cousin said. "They always speak of 'the way out.' They say it is for the weaver and if they don't put it in, something bad might happen to them."

"But they never say death," Rosie added. "*Chindi* pertains only to the dead." She shuddered as she said it, and Alexa, who had heard of the Navajos' renowned distaste for contact with the dead, realized how serious an error the concept of Spirit Trail must be. She made a note. Clarifying this idea would become an important part of her script.

As they drove away from Rosie's, Kurt said, "We have a little time before sunset and I have bread and cheese and some cider in the back. If you don't mind an impromptu picnic, there's something I'd like you to see."

"I'm game," Alexa answered.

Kurt said, "Great!" and turned them toward the road to Flagstaff, then when they reached the highway, said, "Keep your eyes open for highway marker 487."

Alexa began to watch. What she saw was miles of barren desert, red clay, and sand dunes littered with sage and rabbit brush. Dominating it all, visible for miles, was a great, looming wall of red rock to the east. About ten miles from the turnoff, she spotted the marker and Kurt pulled the truck to the roadside. "Now we walk," he said.

The place where they had stopped seemed to be a homestead. A trailer home stood near the road and behind it, a silver water tank. Horses and cattle grazed nearby. "This way," Kurt said, taking her hand. They walked a couple of hundred yards and as they went, the ground fell away beneath them until they stood at the side of a ravine. "There's a natural spring here," Kurt said. "Settlers coming down this way from the Mormon colonies in Utah used to stop here to water their herds, and some left their mark. Come see."

"Is it safe?" she asked, eyes wide.

"The spring comes out right there," Kurt said. "Don't worry. There's no risk of flash floods here."

"Good!" she said, and took his hand.

He helped her down the path into the ravine, where they walked along the sand beside the stream, then picked their way across it. Beyond the water, the sand was strewn with boulders, some of them the size of small cars, and the red wall towered overhead. Alexa found that the people had indeed left their mark. Some of the engravings were recent, such as that made by Virgil and Bertha Howard and their children in 1958. Others were much older and worn by the passage of time. Among them were the names of many early Arizona pioneers, such as Whipple and Hawes. Most of the names were scratched in fairly rude form, but in one place, carefully shaped beveled block letters spelled out a quote from the Book of Psalms: *Oh that men would praise the Lord for his goodness, and for his wonderful works!* On another part of the wall, the same block letters bore the name Reuben Josiah Perkins, Sr.

"Imagine the dedication of these people!" Alexa said as she ran her fingers over the sandstone and some of the scratched-in letters.

"It certainly took commitment," Kurt agreed.

"They gave up everything they had, everything they'd dreamed, to start over. Sometimes it wasn't even their idea. They came because someone else asked them to."

"What do you mean?"

"The early Mormon settlers came because Brigham Young wanted to spread out the Mormon colonies. They were 'called' to Arizona."

The day was warm, but Alexa shivered. Dedication. Commitment. She knew those words, but in the context of pursuing her own dreams. Though she admired the early settlers, she felt more closely allied with the Navajo weavers who always planned their own designs, and always left a pathway out.

Kurt's picnic was simple, but filling, and the magic grew between them as the day wore on. They stopped for the night at two quiet rooms in a clean, if somewhat shabby, motel in Tuba City. Alexa, who had grown used to the intimacy of sleeping in Kurt's old room, still found it disquieting to know that he now slept just through the wall. It didn't help that she was still trembling from their last soul-searing kiss.

On Thursday they drove northward to a hogan Jim knew where a weaver still had some of last year's shearing that had not yet been cleaned and carded. For the camera's eye, she took them through the whole process, right through the spinning of the yarn. Kurt said he had some file footage of Navajos shearing sheep, so they now had a start-to-finish rundown.

"We're winding this up," he said as they headed for home again.

"Good. I'd like to start roughing out the script next week. You and Meg will still want to work on detail and nuance, but I think we can decide on the basic structure before I go." The words were casual when Alexa spoke them, but the expression on Kurt's face was anything but.

"I've been wanting to talk to you about . . ." he began, then seemed to think better of what he had intended, "uh, about tomorrow evening. We're going to be working in the office with Meg most of the day. I thought maybe you and I could host a barbecue at my place tomorrow night and have Meg and Jim over, sort of our way of returning the favor."

"Sounds lovely," she said. "What can I bring?"

The conversation then focused on plans for the coming day and evening, and work they had accomplished in recent days. They climbed the road to Flagstaff, where they pulled the truck off the highway and paused to watch the sun go down. The high forest was already a picture postcard, the season's last snow slowly melting off, majestic trees silhouetted against the brilliant sky. With the colors of the setting sun reflecting off it, the scene was nothing short of splendid.

"Comfortable?" Kurt asked, sliding toward her.

"Not yet," she answered, then met him in the middle of the seat and snuggled close. "Mmm, now I am."

He chuckled, low and throaty. She could have listened to that sound all day.

They sat for a time, watching the sunset and holding each other. The setting was ripe for romance, and Alexa was more than ready when Kurt finally lowered his mouth to hers. She was learning to expect the fireworks—every new kiss had been as potent as the first—but this time there was something new, something she had never felt before. This time the magic went beyond hunger or passion. This time it felt a lot like—

Alexa jerked away, so stunned it must surely be showing on her face. Her breath came in ragged gasps, and she put her hand on Kurt's chest.

"Alexa?" He looked as bewildered as she felt. "Alexa, are you all right?"

She nodded. "Yes, I . . . no . . . that is—"

"Alexa?" he said again, and his look of tender concern seemed to reach inside her and wrap itself around her heart. "I didn't hurt you, did I?"

She managed a weak smile. "No, I'm okay."

"Good." Kurt relaxed a little, but his eyes were ever so serious when he said, "You know I'd never hurt you."

She paused, thinking of Aunt Bobbie's husband, wondering if Danny Sherwood had ever said those words to Lucretia. Deep inside her, she heard the weaver repeating, "*You weave yourself in and there is no way out.*" But the warmth in her heart overwhelmed the voice in her head. She believed him. Whatever else Kurt McAllister was, he was a gentleman. "I know you wouldn't," she answered. When he kissed her again, she gave herself up to it, allowing herself to enjoy the fireworks, letting herself feel the love.

"You like barbecue sauce, Meg?" Kurt called as he turned the meat.

"Yes, please."

"You've got it." *So far, so good,* Kurt thought to

himself. The week had gone well. He was growing more sure of his feelings for Alexa all the time, and she seemed to be sharing in at least some of the more tender moments. Chris had been generally absent the past week, and Alexa hadn't seemed to miss him. That too was a positive sign.

Now she was visiting his home, the two-bedroom fixer-upper on the hill above Holbrook that he'd bought when the business began to pay. He'd done a lot of work on the place and it had become a cozy sanctuary, but it was just a start compared to what he planned. Later this evening, after his other guests left, he hoped to drive Alexa to the acreage he owned on the bluff above Rainbow Rock, there to show her his dreams. Maybe, if good luck followed him, he'd eventually persuade her to share them.

"Okay. The steaks are ready. Let's eat!" he called.

They sat at his outdoor table on the lanai and Alexa slipped quickly into the role of hostess, seeing that the condiments were passed and offering salads and fruit to everyone. He couldn't help thinking what a wonderful wife she'd be, and how much he wanted her to be his.

Little had changed in the three-and-a-half weeks since he'd first seen her—little, and yet everything. He had wanted her then; he only wanted her more now. From the moment he'd first seen her, he'd felt an attraction that was more than chemistry, more than biology. Now he knew it was real. He hadn't known Alexa long, but he knew her well—and what he knew, he loved.

"Oh, dear," Meg said, pushing away from the table.

"What's up, love?" Jim asked.

"This baby never lets me get through a whole meal without at least one bathroom trip," Meg grumbled. "Save my place. I'll be back."

"Hurry," Jim teased. "Your steak looks good."

"There's extra if you're hungry, Jim," Alexa said sweetly as Meg waddled away.

"One more month," Meg said determinedly. "Only one more month." She disappeared inside.

Alexa began telling Jim about their chat with Rosie Nakai's weavers and what she'd learned about the weaver's pathway. Again there was that animated expression that Kurt adored, that passion and enthusiasm that always moved him. He could have sat watching her like that all day. *Enjoy it, McAllister*, he warned himself firmly. *Enjoy it while you can because the lady doesn't plan to be around much longer*. Some part of him knew that caution was necessary, but if the majority ruled, that part would lose. The rest was committed to a plan that would keep Alexa Babbidge by his side for the rest of her life.

"Jim?" Meg was at the door, hunched over like a question mark and clutching at her stomach.

"Contractions again?" Jim asked.

"Yesss," Meg hissed through clenched teeth as a spasm hit her.

Jim hurried quickly to her side and put his arm around her. "Do we need to go home right away, or do you want to finish your dinner first?"

"Neither," she gasped out. "The baby's coming."

Jim paled, but recovered quickly. "We've still got a month to go," he reasoned. "You've had contractions before this—"

"Jim!" Meg snapped. Jim stopped talking and everyone waited. Meg's words were measured when she said, "My water just broke. Ready or not, this baby is coming."

Jim, Kurt, and Alexa all snapped to attention as their quiet dinner collapsed in pandemonium.

Chapter Eight

" "Hello, there. My, aren't you a pretty little thing." Alexa stood at the window of the hospital nursery, tapping on the glass and waving, saying all the silly things people always said to babies who couldn't hear them, and not feeling the least bit foolish.

Meg and Jim's daughter, despite her announcement of an early arrival, had taken her time in coming. It was now mid-morning on Saturday. Alexa and Kurt had paced the waiting room most of the night, along with nervous Uncle Chris. Joan and Bob had called to wish the new parents well and to tell them they'd be over to visit the baby in the morning, and Kate had gone straight through to the labor room to see if she could help.

"She's gorgeous, isn't she?" Jim, still dressed in hospital blues, joined them in the corridor.

138

"She sure is," Kurt said, as proud as if he'd done it all himself. He gave the new papa an awkward embrace and a couple of rough thumps. "She's a knockout, Jim. What're you going to call her?"

"We just decided that a few minutes ago, but I think Meg wants to tell you. Shall we go see her?"

"Is she up to it?" Chris asked.

"She's eager," Jim answered. He looked to Alexa. "Shall we?"

Alexa hesitated, looking at the baby who now stretched and yawned, her mouth a tiny o. "I hate to leave her," she said, then tapped on the glass again. "We waited all night just to see you, didn't we, sweetheart?"

"I've waited a lot longer than that," Jim teased. "Besides, they're going to take the baby into the back to measure and weigh her. We'll be able to see her again in a few minutes."

Alexa smiled. "Then let's go see Meg." She and Kurt and Chris followed Jim down the hall.

Alexa was surprised to see how lovely Meg looked. She'd been there to see her mother after each of the eight births that had followed her own. Although the first ones had been so early she barely remembered them, she recalled the last five or six well, and her mother had always looked beaten and bedraggled. Meg, whose labor had been at least as protracted and difficult, was blooming—her color high, her eyes aglow. "Did you see her?" she asked as they came through her door.

"She's beautiful, Meg," Alexa said, going to the bedside and taking Meg's hand. "She's just beautiful."

"My brother here tells me you were magnificent," Kurt said, stepping next to his mother on the other side. "You always did do good work, partner."

"She's precious, isn't she?" Meg said, glowing at everyone.

"She's perfect," Kate said. "Of course, all my grandchildren are."

"Jim also tells us you've chosen a name," Kurt said, looking pointedly at his partner.

"We have." She looked to Alexa. "If you don't mind, we'd like to call her Alexis. Alexis Katherine, after two of our favorite people."

Alexa felt a rush of warmth. "I'd like that," she whispered, blinking back tears. "I'd like it very much."

"Alexis it is," Jim declared.

They visited a few minutes longer before the nurse came in and suggested the new mother could use some rest. Then Alexa and Kurt accompanied Jim back to the nursery to say good-bye to the baby. They found her lying on her back in the isolette, waving one tiny hand and looking about her with vague, unfocused eyes, frowning as if in concentration.

"She's going to be a bright one, Jim," Alexa said happily. "You won't be able to put anything over on her."

"I'm afraid you're right about that," Jim said, grinning. He'd been grinning every time Alexa had seen him today.

Chris stretched and yawned as widely as the baby had. "Well, I don't know about the rest of you folks, but I think it's time this old uncle caught a nap." He leaned toward the glass. "See you later, sweetheart."

The yawn was infectious. Alexa quickly covered her mouth.

"I think Aunt Alexa is tired too," Jim said. The other two brothers each raised an eyebrow, but neither commented on Jim's use of the word "aunt." "Why don't you all go home and get some rest? You can come back to visit later, if you like."

"That sounds like a good idea," Alexa said.

"I'll give you a lift," Kurt said, taking her elbow.

But the coziness of the words "Aunt Alexa" still rang in her ears. "That's not necessary," she said. "I'll just catch a ride back with Chris, if he doesn't mind?"

She turned to Chris, who seemed discomfited. "Uh, well, that is, I—"

"You two go ahead," Kurt said. "I'll catch a nap and see you later."

"Fine," Alexa said gratefully, then Kurt caught her elbow again.

"Alexa? Can I take you to dinner this evening? There's something I'd like to show you."

She barely hesitated. "Yes, Kurt. I'd like that."

"How's six-thirty sound?"

"Good," she said, and flashed him a quick smile.

Later, as she lay in Kurt's old bed, she drifted rapidly into sleep, into a rest crowded by images of Meg and Jim, so glowingly happy, of her namesake Alexis, of Kurt looking so pleased and proud. Before she awakened, she dreamed that she was the one who had given birth, and that Kurt sat at her bedside, holding her hand and whispering tender endearments as he admired their darling baby girl. She woke with a start and immediately dug through her luggage to reread her résumé. She'd been on her road to Hollywood for a long time; now was the wrong time to be sidetracked by what must surely be a case of female hormones run amok. Still, as the loose threads of her dream drifted about her, she wondered if the treasure she was seeking was worth the one she was giving up.

"We're here," Kurt announced as he parked the truck atop a barren mesa. He got out and walked around to open the door for Alexa.

"And where is here?" she asked, looking around her.

"I told you I wanted to take you to the newest kitchen in Rainbow Rock," Kurt said, removing his Stetson and waving it at the prairie grass. The warm weather had melted the last of March's snows and dried the earth beneath them. "This is it, the newest kitchen in Rainbow Rock—so new it isn't even built yet."

Alexa looked like she didn't know whether to laugh or cry. "Kurt?"

"I told you my little house in Holbrook is a starter home. If the business keeps growing as well as I expect, I can break ground for construction before this summer is out." He walked a few paces and held his arms at full length. "I figure the dining room window should be right about . . . here."

Alexa's eyes widened as she joined Kurt and looked out over a view of the valley and the striped sandstone hills that had earned Rainbow Rock its name. "*This* is where you're building your new home?"

He put his arm around her and drew her close.

"This is it, madam. Would you care to take the grand tour?"

Alexa seemed willing to play along. "Sure. Let's do the tour."

He led her back a few paces. "I think the front entry should go here," he said, "to take advantage of the natural slope of the land to this point."

"Yes," she said soberly. "Good thinking."

"From the entry, we can go straight ahead into the formal living room, to the left into the kitchen—"

"With the dining room beyond," she added.

"Yes, very astute of you to observe that." He wiggled his eyebrows playfully and she laughed. "Or, as you can see, we can step to the near right to go upstairs, or to the far right to go into the office and family room."

"Let's go upstairs," Alexa said, and so he pretended to lead her up a wide staircase and to take her on a tour of the upstairs bedrooms—"four, one for each child"—and the airy upstairs bath. Afterwards, they went downstairs again to tour the family room and living room, with the freestanding fireplace between them, the kitchen and dining room, the pantry, laundry room, and garage. He ended the tour in the huge master suite.

"As you can see," he said, again using the hat to gesture at all he hoped would one day be there, "the master suite is the crowning glory. It has the best view of any room here, especially from the window at this end, a huge bath with a built-in Jacuzzi, and his-and-hers walk-in closets."

"I love the decor," Alexa said, and Kurt was glad she'd gotten into the spirit of his game. "The deep navy and burgundy shades are both relaxing and appealing. With the mix of patterns and textures—''

"—and the oak wainscoting," he added.

"Yes, we mustn't forget the oak wainscoting," she said. "It's really a very lovely room."

She looked so beautiful standing there against the backdrop of the westering sun that Kurt's voice lost something of its playful quality as he said, "Come. See the view."

She stepped beside him and looked down upon the valley with its exquisite painted sands and rounded dunes. The playfulness faded from her voice too. "It's beautiful, Kurt. You're going to have a lovely home here."

"I figure I'll have to fence the back, to give the children a safe place to play without getting too close to the edge of the bluff."

"Good idea," she said.

"But this looks to me like a good place to raise a family."

"Yes," Alexa said, but then her voice grew sad. "A very good place to raise *your* family."

Am I pushing her too hard? he wondered. *Am I imagining it, or did she put extra emphasis on the word "your"—*your *family. I've got less than two weeks. If I don't push now, will I get another chance?* But he didn't dare scare her off. Maybe it was time for a different tack. "Hungry?" he asked. "I've got take-out Thai food and a picnic blanket in the back of the truck."

"Sounds great," she said. They worked together, spreading the blanket and laying out the meal carefully, in Kurt's "dining room." Kurt served and they sat together as the sun set, savoring the delicious blend of flavors and enjoying both the scenery and the breeze. But the magic—and the tension that came with it—hovered about them, reminding them both that their game must soon end.

Kurt repacked the picnic basket, then cozied in beside her. She turned to lean her back against him and he cooperated, giving her his chest as a backrest and wrapping both arms around her waist. For a while they sat still, watching the fading glory of the sunset, seeing the lights go on, one by one, in the valley. After a while, Alexa spoke.

"Is it getting late?" she asked.

"I guess that depends on what you mean by late."

"I'd like to see Meg and the baby again before visiting hours end."

"That still gives us an hour, but we probably should be going soon." He made no move to leave. He was far too comfortable holding Alexa.

"Yes, I suppose we should." It pleased him to see that she didn't move, either. "It was so sweet of them, naming their baby Alexis."

He heard the huskiness in her voice, imagined what might be going through her mind. He hoped she was having second thoughts about leaving, but he didn't want to say that. "Meg is very fond of you," he said. "Jim likes you too, and you have a lovely name. In fact, you're a lovely person."

She turned in his arms to smile up at him. "So are you," she said.

It was an invitation if he'd ever seen one. Kurt held her close and kissed her slowly, thoroughly, trying to put everything he'd ever felt for her into that kiss, hoping to tell her with his actions just how much she had come to mean to him.

She clung to him as meltingly as ever—only this time there was something desperate in the way she drank of his kisses. It was almost as though she was storing all the passionate energy that flowed between them, soaking it up to give her light during dark times ahead. That thought made him deepen the kiss and intensify the embrace, as if he could hold her hard enough to keep her. He didn't stop until he heard a weak moan that sounded more like sorrow than passion. He broke away, breathing raggedly. "I'm sorry. I didn't hurt you, did I?"

She too breathed in ragged gasps. "No, it was just . . . so . . ."

His voice held all the desperation he had felt in her kiss. "We have to talk about this, Alexa. We have to look at what's happening between us."

"Yes," she agreed, but closed her eyes against looking at him, almost as if she couldn't face what she saw in his eyes. "Yes, I know. But not now, Kurt. I can't talk now."

He drew a deep, raspy breath. "When, Alexa?"

"Monday," she said slowly.

"Day after tomorrow?"

"No, the one after that."

"That's cutting it rather close, isn't it?"

She swallowed hard. "Kurt, I need time."

He released her. "Okay, you have it." For a moment, neither of them said anything as their breathing and their heartbeats returned to normal. Then Kurt said, "We'd better be going if we still want to get to the hospital."

"You're right," Alexa said, then helped him fold the picnic blanket and put it in the rear of the truck.

Later, as he watched Meg place little Alexis in Alexa's arms, he couldn't help thinking this was what he'd been missing, what he'd wanted all his life, though he hadn't known it until now: Alexa as his wife, his business partner, his companion, the mother of his children. He could see the years ahead unfolding for them. He could also see the empty, vacant years ahead without her—and a crossroads where the two visions parted.

Nine days. She had given him nine days to sway her decision. *Alexa*, he pleaded with his eyes, *give us a chance, love. Let me give you the life you want, right here with me. Let me show you the end of the rainbow.* She looked up smiling, and he prayed she was reading his mind.

The phone rang. "Good afternoon. Rainbow Productions." Cretia interrupted the office chat that had gone on for nearly an hour. It was Thursday, five days since Alexis's birth, and her mother felt well enough to bring her to the office for a visit. What Meg said she had in mind was a chance to introduce the baby around and look over the script that Alexa had been working on all week. What happened as soon as the three women got together was a long visit about babies and birthing, complete with Cretia's stories of the births of her children, Alexa's tale of little Annie's birth and how she almost had to deliver her baby sister herself, and Meg's own labor experience. They weren't ten minutes into their stories before Kurt announced there was too much estrogen in the room for him, and said he'd be back later.

"Another big order," Cretia announced as she hung up the phone, jotting down the order information.

"That's great!" Meg beamed. "Things are going so well here without me, I'm wondering if I should come back."

"Absolutely, you must," Alexa said. "Kurt will need you even more once I'm gone."

Silence fell in the room. Meg laid her hand over her friend's. "Are you going, Alexa? You know how much we all want you to stay."

"Especially Kurt," Cretia said with a knowing smile.

"Yes, especially Kurt," Meg agreed.

Alexa sighed and rocked her chair back. "I don't know, Meg. The job in California looks like everything I've always wanted. When I left Henderson, I swore I'd given up small-town life forever."

"I know what you mean," Meg said. Then she told Alexa about her own experience going to high school in Rainbow Rock as stepdaughter to the high school principal. "It got pretty nasty sometimes," she said. "I was heavier then and everyone called me Peggy— or Piggy behind my back. I hated it. I swore I'd never come back."

"But you're here," Alexa said.

"I fell in love," Meg answered. "It could happen to you too, Alexa. I know you care about Kurt. Maybe it already has."

"Wait a minute." Alexa's frustration was growing rapidly. "Aren't we assuming a lot here? I mean, Kurt has never said *anything*."

Meg's smile was indulgent. "Hasn't he? Give him half a chance and he'll propose, Alexa. The man is crazy mad in love with you."

The very words seemed to sparkle in the air. "Do you think so?" Alexa asked, sparkling with them, then she shook the idea from her head. "No, he mustn't be! He can't be in love with me, Meg, because I can't stay here." She turned to the other woman. "Cretia, you understand. You know why I have to test my own wings."

Cretia took the cue. "She's afraid of being dependent, Meg," she said. "She has an aunt who got into a difficult marriage and felt stuck there because she didn't have the job skills to support her children without him."

Meg nodded. "I understand, but that will never be a problem for you, Alexa. I've looked at your scripts and they're nothing short of brilliant—clear, concise, packed with valuable ideas."

"That's what I told her," Cretia said.

"But this opportunity with So Fein Productions is a once-in-a-lifetime shot," Alexa argued. "It's my one chance to really make it big, to be someone on my own, and to be financially independent for the first time in my life. I can't let it go, Meg. I can't."

Meg sighed. "If I were you, I might feel the same way. But it'll break Kurt's heart if you go."

Alexa's eyes glittered with tears. "I hope not. I never wanted to do anything to hurt him."

Alexis began to fuss. "I think she's probably hungry," Meg said, checking her watch. "It's probably time to take her home." She turned back to Alexa. "There's just one more thing before I go."

"What's that?" Alexa asked.

"The ability to be financially independent, or independent in anything, doesn't mean you have to choose to be."

Alexa furrowed her brow. "What? I don't understand."

"When you become truly independent, what you're buying for yourself is a choice—a choice to be alone, if that's the way you want to be, or to build healthy, interdependent relationships with other tough, able, independent people. Just because you're *able* to be alone or to work alone, that doesn't mean you have to." She smiled down at Alexis, who was trying to stuff one mittened hand into her mouth. "The best things that have ever happened to me came after I gave up my hard-won independence, knowing that it was my free choice to reach for something higher."

Alexa felt warmed by the words. She reached down to take Alexis' hand, and the baby wrapped tiny mittened fingers around her larger ones. "I understand," she said, her voice low.

"Think about it," Meg said. "Well, come along, daughter." She lifted the baby carrier, and Alexis calmed. "I think we've had enough of the big time for one day."

"See you soon," Alexa said as Meg left the office.

"Think about it," Meg repeated as the door closed behind her.

The phone rang again, and Cretia put her hand on the receiver, but didn't pick it up. "You know, she's right. You're in a position to make a choice I never had. You can choose to be with a man because you want to be—not because you have to."

"Answer the phone," Alexa grumbled.

"Think about it," Cretia coaxed as she lifted the receiver.

By Sunday afternoon, Alexa had thought about little else. She'd enjoyed the church service and the family dinner more than ever, knowing that if she went through with her plans, this would be the last time she would ever join the McAllisters. She had called So Fein Productions on Friday afternoon and the head writer had confirmed their appointment, then told her he was really looking forward to her visit. The end of the rainbow waited for her in Burbank. She'd be a fool to pass it by.

Or would she? As she joined in the singing in Kate's parlor, Kurt wrapped a protective arm about her and held her close. He'd scarcely been farther away than this all week long, and she'd enjoyed his company more than she could say. Though he hadn't yet declared himself, she couldn't help but feel the power of his attention.

And his kisses! She felt certain those kisses were addictive, or fattening at the very least. She'd found another kind of magic with Kurt, a sparkling, shimmering power that could not be denied, and tomorrow night she would meet with him as agreed, facing that power head-on and deciding what to do about it. The unfair part was that she couldn't choose both. This was strictly an either-or decision and she couldn't help feeling that, either way, she was destined to lose.

Kurt stayed late into the evening. In the month that she'd been here, the handsome cowboy who had rescued her on the highway had become a trusted friend and cherished companion, and the closest thing she had ever known to her perfect mate. When he kissed her good night at the door—another of those dazzling, mind-blowing kisses that he didn't seem to mind if the whole family saw—she let him go reluctantly, knowing that tomorrow he would expect her to make a choice.

"That was delicious, Alexa," Kurt said, putting down his fork and scooting his chair away from the table. "I knew you were a fantastic writer, but I didn't know you could cook."

Alexa beamed as she picked up the dishes and took them into Kate's kitchen. Forewarned about Monday's private dinner, Kate and Chris had volunteered to eat in town. "So, are you ready for dessert?" she asked.

Kurt raised his hand in a mock Boy Scout salute. "I solemnly swear I could not eat another bite if my whole life depended on it."

"Not even if it's freshly-baked pecan pie?" Alexa asked.

Kurt groaned. "Oh, how you do tempt me, woman, but it's not pecan pie I'm in the mood for." He caught her hand and dragged her down, laughing, into his lap. "Kiss me," he murmured, and she willingly complied.

Some time later, he lifted his head, then, sighing contentment, finally spoke again. "Alexa, are you ready to talk about us?"

"Yes, I guess." Her voice quavered. "As ready as I'll ever be."

"Okay," he said, then set her on her feet and stood at her side, "but not here. Chris and Mom could come home any minute now."

"Then where?" she asked.

He winked, as if letting her in on a conspiracy. "I know the perfect place for this little chat," he said. "Come with me."

"But the dishes—"

"Leave 'em. I'll help you later."

"Okay." Alexa pulled off her apron with one hand as Kurt led her by the other. Minutes later, they were pulling up on the bare bluff where Kurt's dream house would one day stand.

"Come on," he said, and walked her down to the building pad. There were stakes up, new since the last time they'd been here. When she looked up questioningly, Kurt said, "We break ground May fifteenth. The house should be finished by autumn."

Alexa blinked back shimmery tears; he could only hope they were happy ones. "That's wonderful, Kurt! I'm thrilled for you."

He took a deep breath. As carefully as he'd planned this, he knew it could blow up in his face at any second. "Be thrilled for *us*," he said, then he took both her hands in his. "Alexa, I realize I've been pushing you to talk about us, but I haven't yet told you how I feel. That's why I wanted to come here. I've been trying to *show* you what I feel, but it's not the same as saying it—" He cut himself off. "Heck, I'm making a mess of this."

She stroked his cheek. "Kurt, you don't have to say anyth—"

"Oh, but I do." He paused, then cleared his throat. He'd ridden a Brahma bull once, on a dare, but he'd never been this frightened in his life. "I love you,

Alexa,'' he said, his voice tight. ''I think I've been in love with you since you fell into my arms.''

She smiled; for Kurt, the going got easier. ''During the past month, my feelings have only become deeper, stronger.'' He paused again. ''I brought you up here because this place means so much to me. I know other people long for fame and fortune, Alexa, but for me, this is the pot of gold at the rainbow's end—this right here, family and friends, work I love, a future I can look forward to—and I want to share it with you. I want you to share in my business, my new home, and my life. I want you to be my wife and the mother of my children.'' While he still had his courage up, he dropped to one knee and brought out the jeweler's box he had hidden so carefully at the office for the past few days. ''Alexa, will you marry me?''

''Oh, Kurt,'' she said. She was crying as she took the jeweler's box into her hands. She opened it, gasped, and began crying harder.

He'd known the ring was meant to be hers the moment he saw it, just as he'd known somehow that she was meant to be his. It had cost him more than he'd intended to spend, but it was worth it all to see the look on her face right now—if only she wasn't crying.

''Oh, Kurt!'' she said again, and put both arms around him, kissing him with a fervor unlike any he had ever felt—except on the last time they had come here, when her kiss had been so desperate. She drew away from him and the tears ran unheeded down her cheeks as she said, ''You darling, darling man. I love you too.''

Skyrockets weren't powerful enough to describe his elation. He bent to catch her around the waist, but she stopped him, snapped the ring box shut, and slipped it into his shirt pocket.

"I love you," she said again, "but . . ."

He saw the haunted look in her exquisite eyes. "But you're going," he finished, his voice flat.

Her tears were pouring now. "I've never lied to you, Kurt. From the beginning I've told you where I was going and what I planned to do."

"I know," he said, gulping out the words over the fist-sized stone that had just lodged in his throat.

"I'm so sorry." She reached to stroke his face again, but he lifted her hands away.

"When will you go?"

"First thing in the morning."

"So soon?"

"Under the circumstances . . ."

"Okay, I see." He felt his arms and hands go rigid. It was all he could do to avoid yelling, or clobbering something. "I guess I'd better drive you back now." They were silent on the trip back to his mother's house. When they got to the door, Kurt knew he couldn't draw this out. "Do you mind if I don't stay to help with the dishes?"

"No. I don't mind." Alexa looked as dejected as he felt.

"Good-bye, Alexa," he said, dropping a quick kiss on her cheek, then driving away before he made an even greater fool of himself.

Alexa watched until the last wisps of dust had disappeared, tears dampening her face and neck and collar. Despite Meg's warning, she'd never imagined that Kurt planned to propose, that he would offer her a diamond the size of a pomegranate seed, that he'd ask her to be the mother of his *children*, for heaven's sake! He had looked so dear, so perfectly wonderful kneeling there on the bluff, his heart in his eyes, and she had known then that she loved him as much as she'd probably ever love anyone. If there had been even a glimmer of the life she had planned for herself in the dreams he'd laid before her, she could have sacrificed her old dreams to embrace tender new ones. But she wasn't like the early pioneers who had left their lives behind to colonize Arizona because of their faith in another's vision, and Kurt's dreams weren't like the carefully planned designs of Rosie Nakai. The tapestry he had woven before her was complete, tightly contained and fully bordered. There wasn't so much as a single thread to be her pathway out.

"Well, the die is cast now," she said aloud, silently praying that she'd made the right choice. She started in the kitchen, halfheartedly cleaning up the mess she had made only hours before, hoping that beef Stroganoff and pecan pie would set the right mood. The pie had never even been cut. Wiping tears to avoid ruining it, she shoved it into the refrigerator for Kate and Chris, then went upstairs to pack.

Before the next sunrise, she was on the road. She left a note on the table for Kate to find and a second for Meg. A third, addressed to Kurt, said only, *Please forgive me.* That done, she drove away without looking back. She was past Holbrook on I-40, near the exit for Cholla Lake, when the tears finally overwhelmed her and she could no longer see to drive. She took the exit and parked near the lake until she had sobbed out the worst of it, then solemnly dried her tears.

Something caught her eye. As she turned and looked back at the eastern hills, dawn broke over Rainbow Rock. A light rain was falling and the Rainbow Goddess had come, spreading her joy across the earth. Alexa could have sworn that the rainbow ended right over Kurt's hill. "Good-bye, Kurt," she choked. "I love you." Then she drove away without a backward glance.

Chapter Nine

A hot Santa Ana wind scrubbed the Los Angeles basin, snatching puffs of brownish smog and drifting them above the ubiquitous palm fronds. Alexa watched the clearing with idle pleasure, sourly reminded of her mother's halfhearted attempts at spring cleaning.

It had been a great production meeting at the studios that morning. If all went as planned, So Fein Productions would soon contract for a new one-hour dramatic series to follow "Mountain Magic" on Wednesday evenings. Alexa's role as a member of the writing team was well established. Her episode involving native mountain crafts, which had aired last week, was already being rumored as a front-runner for an award, and she had just placed a treatment with a major studio that might get her a contract for a movie as well. In the five months since she had arrived in Burbank,

Alexa had built a portfolio of successful scripts that
were already bringing in high market shares for her
program. She was earning a strong reputation in the
business and had recently moved to a townhouse
apartment in an attractive area of Sherman Oaks. All
was going splendidly, better than expected.

So why, Alexa wondered as she gunned the engine
of her shiny new sportscar and pulled into the fast lane
on 101 West, did she feel like pounding the stuffing
out of something large and inanimate?

Fearing that she knew the answer, she forced herself
to take several deep breaths. *Alexandra Cozette, calm
down*, she chided herself. *You've just been working
too hard lately. That's all that's the matter with you.
You need to have some fun.* She did her best to believe
it as she saw the taillights flash on ahead of her, and
slowed to a thirty-mile-per-hour crawl.

Traffic continued to slow—her punishment, she decided, for letting herself leave early enough to catch
the end of the evening rush—and soon she was caught
in the stop-and-go, bumper-to-bumper, used-car-lot
traffic of the L.A. basin. Fearing she'd hurt something
if she let her agitation reign, she chose to focus instead
on the upcoming evening, and her date.

Riley Duncan was one of the hottest new stars on
television. At least the fan mags and billboards all said
so. Attractive as sin, with black hair and blue eyes and
a body to die for, he was charming the wits out of
half the women in Hollywood, but it was Alexa he
had asked to dinner this evening. As the male lead on
''Mountain Magic,'' he had worked closely with her
during recent months. She had suggested that he take
on a more ''native'' look, and by the third fall episode

he was appearing in buckskins. She had given his character, Isaiah Stone, an increasingly important role in the life of the series' main character. Along the way, she'd learned to like Riley, and he appeared to like her too. This evening they were going to an exclusive, upscale dinner club. If all went well, sexy Riley Duncan might just be the one to rid her dreams of a certain hunky blond cowboy who could still raise her heart rate just by smiling from her memories.

"Um-hm. Sounds good." Kurt sat at his desk, not quite hearing Meg's rundown on the day's mail, and idly stacking paper clips.

"Kurt, can't you even pretend to listen?"

The irritation in Meg's voice finally got his attention. "Sorry, sis. What were you saying?"

"I'm telling you, you dear man with a vacancy above your eyebrows, that we may be nominated for an award. A *film award,* Kurt! Can you believe that? Our contact at PBS says we're the talk of all the trade magazines." She looked as thrilled as she was dumbfounded.

He stared as if she'd just grown a second head. "An award? You mean, an award from a film festival? How? For what?"

"*The Weaver's Way*, of course. It may be a nominee for best documentary of the year."

He felt the impact just above his sternum. *The Weaver's Way. Alexa.* He couldn't think her name without hurting. Before the ides of March, he hadn't even known she existed. Then a terrible, wonderful, amazing month had made her a part of his life, so completely that even her desertion hadn't changed it.

Five months later, he still wanted her as much as ever. But Meg was watching him, waiting for his response. "No wonder," he said carefully. "It's the best work we've ever done."

"Absolutely," she agreed. Then she laughed, practically hopping up and down. "An award, Kurt! I'm going to go tell Jim."

"Have a good time," he said as she stood.

"Physician, heal thyself," Meg quoted. "It's about time you got out and had a little fun."

"Yeah, yeah. I've heard it before," he grumbled.

Meg picked up her jacket. "I mean it, Kurt. Call somebody and make a date. Or maybe your brothers and I should make one for you?"

He held up his hands as if warding off a blow. "Heaven forbid!"

"Then call somebody," Meg said as she reached the door. "Splurge a little. Celebrate. Can't hurt, can it?"

Kurt managed a weary smile. Hurt was probably all it could do. Still, he'd always been a believer in getting back up on the horse that threw you, and it *had* been five months. Maybe it was time. He picked up the phone, determined to think of someone he could call.

By the time the server asked if they'd like coffee or dessert, Alexa was ready to run for the door. The restaurant was lovely, the food delicious, the ambience charming, and the music delightful. Taken altogether, Alexa would have had more fun scrubbing her kitchen floor.

Who would have thought it? Sexy Riley Duncan

was a self-involved, gold-plated bore. For nearly two hours, Alexa had listened to him rattle on about how Isaiah should start doing more woodcutting scenes that would allow him to appear without a shirt. "He needs more screen time," Riley had said at least six times, "and you ought to heat up the romance between Isaiah and Claire."

"Remember this is the turn of the century," Alexa reminded. "We can't heat it up much if we're going to be authentic."

Riley's smile was smug and self-assured. Alexa hated to think of the opportunities that smile had probably bought him. "People don't want authentic," he drawled, then leaned across the table as if to kiss her. In her startled withdrawal, Alexa upset her water glass and they spent the next minute repairing the damage.

As they left the restaurant, Riley asked if she'd like to prolong the evening. Alexa answered that it had been a big week and she thought she'd like to go right home, and Riley responded with that same smug, self-satisfied grin. Alexa wondered irritably if it would take more than one slap to wipe it from his face. At her door she hurried things along, telling him she'd had a nice time and would see him on Monday.

"Aren't you going to ask me in?" he asked.

"Not this time," she said, trying to manage a smile. She already had the door unlocked and her hand on the doorknob, but she wasn't fast enough. Riley grabbed her with a kiss so fierce it knocked the breath out of her. It was a punishing kiss, meant to reprove her for not inviting him in, and it lasted for some time, while Alexa pushed at his chest, trying to break away. His embrace could only be described as passionate, his kiss skillful, but in her mind's eye, Alexa saw the Kiss-o-Meter from her dream registering a flat line. When she finally broke free, she pushed through her door and slammed it, then leaned against it and slowly slid down until she sat on the floor, her eyes moist with frustration.

She'd just been kissed by the man the tabloids touted as ''Sexiest in America'' and all she had wanted was to end it as quickly as possible.

It was Saturday morning and Kurt showed up at his mother's house just in time for pancakes and eggs. Unperturbed, Kate asked how many he wanted and put on the blueberry syrup he preferred as well as the maple she kept for Chris, then told him to set himself a place at the table and get the milk and butter while he was at it.

When they had eaten, Chris went out to work with the pigs and Kate handed Kurt a fresh dish towel. ''Too few to run the dishwasher,'' she explained as she put a wet plate into his hands. ''So what's on your mind?''

''Can't I just drop by for breakfast now and then?''

''Sure, but you never do.'' Kate waited for a response. When Kurt remained silent, she said, ''I saw you in town with Mitzi Lewis last night.''

Kurt's only answer was a noncommittal grunt.

''She's a nice girl.''

Still no response.

''Too bad she's not for you.''

Kurt rose to the bait. ''Why do you say that? Mitzi's great.''

Kate smiled. ''Of course she is. She's lovely, sings

like an angel, beautiful, gentle . . ." She paused and cast Kurt a slanting glance. ". . . compliant. . . ."

Kurt's eyes narrowed. "What are you trying to say, Mom?"

Kate set down her iron pancake griddle and put her hands on her hips. "Don't play dumb, Kurt. Mitzi Lewis is as sweet as they come, but she hasn't had an original thought in her life. You'd be bored with her inside a year."

Kurt felt his face reddening. "Yeah, well, I listened to all the stuff you told me when I first started dating Cretia Sherwood, all about how I should pick a bright, intelligent, *independent* woman with dreams and ideas of her own. Look where that got me."

Kate's look gentled. "Have you heard anything from Alexa?"

Kurt blew out a sigh. "Not a word."

Kate laid a hand on her son's arm. "She's the only kind of woman worthy of you, son."

"Yeah, well, she followed those dreams and ideas of hers right to California. Do not pass go, do not collect Kurt McAllister."

"And what did you offer her to stay?" Kate asked gently.

"Everything!" Kurt realized he'd spoken louder than he meant to. "Sorry. I offered her everything, Mom. A share in the business, a dream home, a whole life."

Kate lifted her chin. "*Your* business, *your* dream home, *your* life. Did you leave her anything of her own, Kurt? Or did you expect her to give up everything she wanted to become a part of you?"

"Ouch." Kurt winced and sank into a kitchen chair.

He was remembering the day they'd gone to the pioneer carvings together, and Alexa's fascination with the weaver's pathway. She had written the concept into a brilliant script that might one day earn his company an award—and he had never seen what it meant to her. "I guess you're right. She needed a pathway," he murmured. "Maybe that was *all* she needed."

Kate looked perplexed. "A pathway?"

Kurt felt crushed. "It doesn't matter now."

Kate smiled mysteriously, "You never know." Then she shook out her dishrag and seemed to change the subject. "You know, Meg's been writing a lot of letters lately."

Kurt stared at his mother. Had she lost her mind?

"Personal letters. Some to California."

He slowly came to his feet, his face registering astonishment, then hope. "Are you saying . . . what I think you're saying?"

"You never know," Kate said again, and grinned broadly.

Her letter carrier was just leaving the mailbox when Alexa came home from her weekly grocery trip. There were a couple of bills, a pair of ad circulars, and three letters, including one from the film producers who were considering her treatment. She opened it first, then whooped with delight at the opening lines. The executive producer wrote that her ideas "had the makings of a highly successful project" and suggested they meet for contract negotiations. He even hinted that he might want her to write the screenplay, although he said they'd like to go ahead with their own studio writers if she was too busy with "Mountain

Magic.'' Either way she'd get major credits and a piece of the pie. She felt like dancing.

Still glowing from the producer's news, she opened the letter from home. Her mother wrote that the new roof had been put on last week, then thanked Alexa for the microwave oven and food processor. She sent greetings from the two brothers who were in college now, thanks to Alexa's tuition checks, and assured her that everyone was delighted with their new school clothes. She also enclosed a picture of the newly painted farmhouse.

Alexa sighed in satisfaction. Financial independence was at least as good as she'd hoped it would be, and ''Mountain Magic'' had been better to her than she'd dreamed. Already she had her own agent, accountant, and stockbroker—and money in the bank, obscene stacks of it. If the movie deal went well— She cut off the thought. Money was nice, very nice, but it wasn't the end of the rainbow. That vague, uncertain, unfulfilled feeling that had been driving her for years hadn't diminished in the least, despite the new car, the chic apartment, the growing investment portfolio. Even her gifts to the folks back home hadn't filled the void.

Feeling dejected despite her great news, Alexa dropped to the couch, shored up her courage, and opened the third letter. It took fortitude to read the regular missives that came from Meg. This one started with the business, bubbling to Alexa about the grand success of *The Weaver's Way* and how Rainbow Productions would have the rights to sell it to home subscribers after it appeared on network television. It then went on to talk about how cute Alexis was getting (the letter included four snapshots), how she was start-

ing to pull herself with one arm and would soon be
crawling, and how everyone missed Alexa and hoped
she'd stop back for a visit soon.

The letter went on to talk about Cretia and how well
she was doing in the business. She had taken over all
the order filling and restocking and was becoming an
efficient, vital part of Rainbow Productions. Meg was
clearly pleased with the result. *"We owe that to you,"*
she wrote, *"and we want you to know how much we
appreciate it."* That "we" was the only mention in
the letter—the only mention in any of Meg's letters—
of the one McAllister who interested Alexa most.

Deciding she'd put off an answer for another time,
Alexa put the letters on her desk and started unloading
groceries. Meg's positive, upbeat letters always meant
so much to her, but writing an answer in kind was
going to take more energy than she had just now.
Maybe she'd write next week, after her meeting at the
movie studios.

Kurt waited until both Meg and Cretia were well
started on the morning's work. It was Tuesday and he
had been pondering his mother's words for several
days now. Sometime in the early-morning hours, in
the middle of another near-sleepless night, he'd finally
decided what he needed to do.

"Meg, do you have a minute?" he asked, trying to
keep his voice nonchalant.

"Sure. What do you need?"

"May I see you in the back room?"

Meg raised an eyebrow, then checked on Alexis,
who slept in her travel seat, and said, "Sure. Let's
go."

Ten minutes later, Kurt emerged from the storage room with a slightly confused, very happy sister-in-law and a card containing the mailing address of a certain hot-as-a-brushfire scriptwriter. He'd asked for the phone number as well, but Meg explained she didn't have it.

Asking careful, tentative questions, he then caught up on the details of Alexa's life—at least, as much as she was willing to tell Meg. He learned there was apparently no one new to distract her memories, and things seemed to be going splendidly for her in California, though her letters frequently mentioned being lonely and "missing everyone." Everything he learned gave him hope. Now all he needed was the courage to write Alexa and tell her about his new, updated plan. He hoped it wasn't too little, too late.

Alexa left the studios with her head in the clouds. The hottest producers in Hollywood were backing her project, and they were so impressed with her ideas that they planned to give her fairly extensive creative control—and a sizable chunk of the picture's gross. She'd known that a movie that dealt sensitively with Native American issues would have a good chance, what with the political climate in Hollywood these days, but she'd never imagined this kind of response! It was dizzying.

She pulled up at a stoplight on a Burbank surface street and waited for the light to turn green. As she sat, pondering the choices that lay before her, the lawn sprinklers went on at the corner building. In the circular spray from one nozzle, Alexa saw a rainbow. With a start, she realized she hadn't seen a rainbow in all the months she'd been in California. Why, the last one she'd seen had been—

She gasped as a stab of longing struck with an almost physical impact. "Oh, Kurt!" she sobbed. It was as if a dam had broken inside her, releasing a flash flood of memories: the Rainbow Goddess, the end of the rainbow touching down on Kurt's hill; Kurt's face as he asked her to spend her life with him; his gentle hands as he held her near the rushing water; the tears she had shed as she sat parked at Cholla Lake; the exquisite rugs, their tiny threads of pathway reaching toward her like miniature lifelines.

The car behind her honked and Alexa realized the light had changed. She pressed forward, barely seeing the road through a veil of shimmery tears.

Later that evening, she picked up her phone and called Meg, who seemed both surprised and delighted to hear her voice. Ten minutes later, through a series of careful, tentative questions, she had caught up on the details of Kurt's life—at least, as much as Meg knew. She'd learned that apparently there was no one new to distract Kurt's memories, and that things seemed to be going splendidly for Rainbow Productions and for its handsome co-owner, though Meg said he frequently seemed lonely. Everything she learned gave her hope.

She said good-bye, then pulled out the paperwork from the morning's meeting and called her agent at home. It took only a short while to confirm her reading of the meeting. The producers had offered her the chance to do the whole screenplay, and they were willing to put cash on the line to make it happen. If she would consider leaving "Mountain Magic". . . She blew out a deep breath. Only five months ago the idea of working on ''Mountain Magic'' had been the most exciting life she could imagine. It was hard to believe that she had found a possibility with even greater potential, both professionally and personally.

''Mountain Magic'' had also taught her that Meg was right. She'd been more independent since her arrival in Burbank than ever in her life, but the award-winning program was not the result of independence, but of *inter*dependence—of talented, able, creative people working together, from the producers and directors, through the writers and actors, right on down through set designers, prop directors, and makeup artists, even the custodians who kept the set clean and the production assistants who fetched coffee. She was getting a lot of accolades lately for the episode that might yet win her that dream Emmy, but that episode hadn't resulted from her toughness and independence, nor had the script arisen from her painful aloneness. They had come, as Meg assured her all great things did, from mutual involvement with others, and she had to realize that one of the most significant others had been Kurt.

Interdependence was working well for her in her professional life; now if she could only get it going in her personal life . . . Alexa jumped up, eager to put her new plan into action.

Kurt hung up the phone and put his head into his hands. He'd been trying for three hours to track down Alexa's unlisted phone number, and he was having no luck. Now it looked like, unless he was willing to take the time to drive to southern California—something the business simply couldn't afford—he was probably going to have to talk to her in a letter, and that was just a bit impersonal for what he had in mind.

He looked up as the bell on the front door rang. "Hey, bro!" he greeted Chris as he entered.

"Hey, yourself." Chris reached into his pocket. "I have something for you." He tossed a three-by-five note card onto Kurt's desk.

"What's this?"

Chris grinned. "What's it look like?"

Kurt examined the card. All it contained was a list of numbers starting with area code 213. "Aha!" Kurt grinned. "Thanks, man. I owe you one."

"Just remember to name that boy of yours after me," Chris said. He winked as he went out the door.

Alexa entered the offices of So Fein Productions with her letter of resignation in hand, dropped it on the head writer's desk, then went looking for Don to tell him what she'd just done. When she found him in the company lounge, he was surprisingly understanding and even admitted that he'd take the same opportunity if he could. Looking at her earned vacation, he told her she could leave early if she'd just work out the week and finish the episode she was writing.

Later that evening, she went through her apartment, organizing her things and musing about Kurt. She knew she had hurt him badly. Her whole plan hinged on the hope that he had a truly forgiving nature, and remembering what had happened with Cretia, Alexa felt encouraged. Still, it was the biggest gamble of her life. She could only hope that her mind could relax and enjoy the directions her heart was taking her.

*   *   *

After three calls to her apartment, at different hours of the evening, Kurt knew Alexa was lost to him. If there'd been any hope at all, wouldn't she be home at *some* hour of the night? It had been almost two weeks since he'd first thought of this, and it had taken this long to think it through. Maybe he'd simply waited too long. He hung up in frustration, sorry he'd allowed himself to hope. Still, by midday on Thursday, the hope had surfaced again, encouraging him not to give up until he'd tried Alexa's office. Taking a deep breath and crossing his fingers—not so much for luck as for courage—he dialed the number.

"So Fein Productions. May I help you?"

Somehow he hadn't expected a secretary. "Alexa Babbidge, please."

"I'm sorry, sir, but Ms. Babbidge is no longer with this company."

His heart sank. He barely managed to mumble something appropriate and get the phone back into its cradle. He'd been a fool—not once, but twice, at least—and it had cost him the love he'd longed for.

Mumbling something incoherent to Cretia, he stumbled out of the office and drove to his hill, to the place where his dreams had first been shattered. There was no house here. After Alexa's desertion, he hadn't had the will to go through with building it. Then when he'd planned to call her again . . . well, that didn't matter now. He put his head down on the steering wheel and sat—alone. Before Alexa, he had never felt this lonely. Since Alexa, he'd seldom felt anything but.

He looked heavenward. "If this is love," he said meaningfully, "it's a bad idea." Then he sat till twilight shadowed the hill.

Chapter Ten

It was almost five o'clock and Cretia, who had come in early to fill the backlog of new orders, was itching to see her children. "Can you believe it? They're already looking at Halloween costumes," she said. "If you don't mind, I'd like to pick them up before the stores close."

"Sure, go ahead," Kurt encouraged. "I'll see you Monday."

Meg had left more than an hour ago, eager to get Alexis into a more comfortable setting before the first snowfall of the season, which already threatened in the lowering sky. In his desultory mood, Kurt thought it fitting that he should once again be alone.

Cretia waved as she went out and Kurt sighed and put his head down on his desk. He'd slept little since his sad vigil on the hill the night before. He was exhausted, far beyond a normal need for rest, but sleep would probably elude him tonight as well. He was too full of sad memories—and bitter regrets.

If only, he had thought a thousand times. If only he had seen Alexa as she was—whole, complete, an individual in her own right with every much as great a need as he felt for dreams and plans and personal fulfillment. If only he had recognized her fear of sacrificing everything. If only he'd read her needs and offered her the right to make decisions for herself. Somehow he had foolishly believed his dreams were big enough for both of them. Then when she left, he had blamed her solely, certain she was the one who was making the mistake, and never realizing the terrible mistake he had made. *Never assume*, he reminded himself, wishing he'd remembered the axiom a few months earlier.

Deciding to check the inventory on mail-order copies of "The Weaver's Way," more popular than ever since it had aired on PBS, he stepped into the back room, and was surprised to hear the bell ring as the front door opened.

Who could that be? he asked himself. Since their business was primarily by telephone and mail order, the front door was seldom used except when he or Meg or Cretia went to lunch, and it was too late for the mail. "Just a moment," he called and stepped into the office. Then he took one look at the door and nearly dropped over from shock. "Alexa?"

"Hi," she said, awkwardly holding her purse in front of her.

He gulped. "What are you doing here?"

She took a deep breath, trying to locate the courage

that had fled at Kurt's cool reception. "Gee, Kurt, it's good to see you too."

He shook his head as if clearing a haze. "Sorry. It's just . . . I never expected to see you again." For a moment they stared at each other, then Kurt finally forced himself into action. "May I take your coat? Would you like to sit down?"

"Yes," she said. "That would be nice."

He removed her expensive, beautifully tailored jacket, careful not to touch her, then hung her wrap on the coat tree and offered her the chair she had once used. "You're looking well," he said, feeling as inane as he probably sounded.

In fact, she looked marvelous. Southern California, for all its ills, had apparently agreed with Alexa. Her skin shone with a fresh glow of health, and her sky eyes sparkled. Her hair had grown since he'd seen it last, and she'd combed it differently, letting a soft tendril fall over each shoulder. Her peach-colored jumpsuit clung becomingly in all the right places and emphasized her slim waist and feminine curves. It was all he could do to keep from sweeping her into his arms.

Kurt sighed, reminding himself that he had no rights here. Once, they'd been so close, but that had been some time ago. All these observations and thoughts flashed through his mind in a moment, and he barely remembered the comment he'd made when she responded, "Thank you. So do you."

Alexa couldn't help thinking what a magnificent understatement that was. Riley Duncan, in his hottest magazine-cover pose, could never look as good as Kurt McAllister did just sitting here, tired at the end of a long day, his beard beginning to come in thick and blond. No one had ever stirred her blood as he did, either.

She sat staring at him, drinking in the sight, and feeling as shell-shocked as he looked. She could only hope her plan to come here had been a good idea, but looking at the expression on Kurt's face, she was beginning to wonder. Was it possible she'd made a terrible mistake? If she had, it wasn't her first.

"May I get you something to drink?" he asked, casting about for something to say. "I don't have much here in the office, but I could get you some cold water." He started to stand. "I may even have soda in the back."

"No, thanks." She held out her hand to stop him. Their hands brushed. To Alexa, it felt like an electric shock.

Kurt felt it too, and slowly sat down again. He saw the look in her eyes, the same longing that must surely be showing in his. "How have you been?" he asked.

Alexa smiled, glad to put the conversation on a more personal footing. "Good," she said. "Happy, successful, busy." She paused and bit her lip. "Lonely."

He nodded. "Me too." Then he reached forward, watching her eyes for permission as he took her hand.

She happily gave it. She'd come a long way to make this work. "Did you finish your house?" she asked.

He shook his head. "Didn't even start it. My plans sort of . . . changed."

She flinched. "I'm sorry, Kurt. I never wanted to hurt you."

"I know," he said. Then somehow they were in

each other's arms, holding each other, clinging desperately as if the last months had been little more than a sad dream. "It was my fault," he said when the emotion cleared enough to let him speak again. "It was all my fault."

She looked at him with amazement. "What was your fault? I'm the one who left."

"But I gave you little choice. I didn't even see that until my mother pointed it out to me. I wanted you to live my life, and I never made any room in my plans for yours." He grimaced. "Are all men as dumb as I am?"

"Oh, no," she said, so happy to be in his arms again that the words scarcely mattered. "Some are much dumber."

He chuckled, but quickly sobered. "Alexa, I was a fool. I offered you everything I had, not even realizing you had dreams of your own. I was wrong to assume that my dreams would be big enough for both of us." He paused. "I called you yesterday."

"You did?" She could hardly believe her ears. All those weeks she had jumped every time the phone rang, hoping to hear Kurt's voice, and he had finally called her *yesterday?*

He was watching her face, and apparently reading her mind again. "Yeah. Slow, huh?"

"A little," she admitted, still stroking his back, touching his shoulders, assuring herself he was real.

"I wanted to ask you to come back. I wanted to tell you that I'll redesign the house the way you want it, give you room to do the things you want to do, make space in my life for your dreams too. I love you, Alexa. I'm so sorry I ever let you go."

He kissed her then, and Alexa practically sobbed with relief, but Kurt seemed as glad to see her as she was to see him, and the kiss rated at least a nine on her ten-point Kiss-o-Meter scale. "I'm sorry I left," she answered as they parted, "but I almost had to, Kurt. I wish I could explain to you what it meant to me to give myself that chance."

"I think maybe I understand it—now." He cleared his throat. "Meg tells me you've been doing very well."

She frowned. "You've been talking to Meg? All this time and you never—"

"Whoa! Back up! I didn't know Meg was in touch with you until about a week ago. She never said a word and I thought you'd disappeared without leaving an address."

"Oh," Alexa said, mollified. "So what has she told you?"

"Just that you're doing great and they're paying you well." He chewed his lip, looking like a school-boy caught with a frog in his shirt pocket. "I don't know if it's macho to admit this, but I watch 'Mountain Magic' every week. It's probably the finest program on television."

She beamed, more warmed by his praise than by the highest honors of the toughest critics. "I'm glad you like it."

Encouraged, he went on. "I especially liked the episode about the native mountain crafts. It reminded me of the work we did together on the weaving tape."

"I wrote that one," she said proudly. "And I was thinking of the weavers when I did it. My producers—that is, *the* producers—think it might win an award."

"Congratulations," he said, pleased to realize that he was sincerely happy for her. Then a thought dawned. "Wouldn't it be something if you won two awards in the same year?"

"Two awards?" she asked, wondering what he knew about her film deal, and knowing that the movie wouldn't hit the screens for a couple of years.

Kurt told her then about the letter Meg had opened and about the critical acclaim that had greeted *The Weaver's Way*. Alexa's expressive face responded with shock, then wonder, then delight. "That's wonderful, Kurt. I'm glad it's doing so well."

They chatted about the business, then Kurt risked a tentative question. "Are you back for a visit, Alexa? If so, for how long?"

"I'm not sure. I've been thinking about an offer you made some time ago," she began. "You said if I ever wanted a scriptwriter's job, there'd be one open for me here."

"Here?" he asked, stunned. "You're willing to leave the hottest show on television to come . . . *here?*"

"Yes, if you still want me to."

Kurt's brow furrowed as he pinned her with his gaze. "Why, Alexa?"

Her lip trembled. She shored up her courage and went for it. "Because my life has been full of everything I ever wanted, and so empty I sometimes cry myself to sleep. Because I saw a rainbow in a lawn sprinkler and suddenly knew I was going in all the wrong directions. Because I'm so madly, wildly, feature-special in love with you that I can hardly see straight. Because—"

"Whoa!" Kurt looked bewildered, but happily so. "Run that by me again, without the rainbows."

Happy tears filled her eyes. "Kurt, I'm in love with you. I knew it before I left here, but I still felt I had to try for my dreams. Now I have it all, everything I've ever dreamed of, and it isn't what I want at all. I need you in my life too, that is, if you still want me."

"If I still want . . ." He shook his head at the thought. "Alexa, I've never in my life wanted anything so much." He drew her into an embrace designed to prove just how much.

"About that scriptwriting job?" she said as they came out of the embrace. "I want to make it clear that I'm only interested in part-time employment. I have a contract to write a screenplay for one of the biggest production houses in Hollywood and I'll need some time away from the office to work on it. At least four hours a day."

Kurt grinned. "Rainbow Productions will be proud to have your talents, Ms. Babbidge, even on a minimal part-time basis."

"And that's another thing," Alexa said, taking courage from the power of Kurt's kiss. "The name, I mean. I heard there might also be an opening for a Mrs. Kurt McAllister. That is, unless there's another candidate for the job?"

Kurt swallowed hard, barely daring to believe what he was hearing. "No," he rasped. "No other candidates. The job's still open."

"Then I'd like to apply for that one also," she said, "on a full-time basis, please, though I'd prefer to keep Babbidge for professional purposes."

Kurt was smiling so hard his face hurt. "Sounds great to me."

"There's one other thing," Alexa said. "That house on the hill that you haven't started building yet. Do you think it could be ready in time for a December wedding?"

December? As soon as December? Kurt felt dizzy from the joy of it. "December might be a little soon," he said. "That's only a couple of months, but I think we could push it. On the other hand, what do you think of January fourth?"

"It means waiting longer," Alexa said with a pretty pout. "Why January fourth?"

"It was my parents' wedding anniversary."

Alexa nodded. "January fourth it is."

"And about the house. That's the reason I called you yesterday. I've put my plans away. Assuming you're still interested in living there, I'd like you to design our home. And if that site isn't what you want, I can put it on the market tomorrow."

"Oh, no, don't sell it!" she cried. "That's the perfect place for a dream home—and your design is great too. There's only one thing I want to change."

Kurt didn't know whether to feel delighted or concerned. "What's that?"

"Those four bedrooms upstairs—one for each of the children?"

"Yup."

"Let's keep the four rooms as planned, but make it one for each of the children, plus a guest room and a study."

Understanding dawned, and he smiled. "The girl

from the big family doesn't want a big family of her own?'' he guessed.

She sharpened her voice. "Listen, cowboy. From where I'm standing, two looks like a plenty big family."

He chuckled. "I can live with that."

"And I get to invest a part of my income and manage my own investments," she added, trying to remember all the pathways she had woven into her plans.

He nodded. "I can live with that too, as long as I'm a joint tenant in everything. You'll be a joint owner in all the investments I manage."

"That's fair," she agreed. "I'll also have to do some traveling, especially when a project is filming. I may even have to do some on-location work, sometimes for a week or more. Oh, and when I'm on deadline with a screenplay, I won't be available for Rainbow Productions at all."

He thought she looked defiant, as if she expected an argument. "I'm a filmmaker," he said. "I can understand that. But let's plan schedules ahead so we stagger your projects with Rainbow's."

"That's reasonable. And the part about traveling? You can live with that too?"

He nodded. "Yeah, though I reserve the right to grouse about being lonely when you're gone, and to visit you on site if you're gone too long."

Alexa drew another deep breath, knowing she had just negotiated the biggest deal of her life, knowing also that they had woven it carefully, planning their own pathways and making room for each other in the pattern. "Great," she said, finally content. "Then we have a deal. Shall we shake on it or something?"

He shook his head. "Ms. Babbidge, I think that's the oddest proposal I ever heard." He moved toward his desk. The ring was still there, in the back of the drawer. He hadn't been able to look at it since that night on the hill, not even to take it back to the jeweler's. "There's just one part of the deal we haven't settled."

This time it was Alexa who raised her eyebrows. "And what's that?"

"Will you love me forever, live with me for the rest of our lives, and tell me when I'm being an insensitive jerk?"

She smiled. "I like that. Shall we make it part of the formal vows?"

"Oh, and one more thing. If one of those two children happens to be a son, I want to name him—middle name, at least—after my brother Chris. Can you live with that?"

"Happily," she agreed.

"Then there's only one thing left to do." He dropped to one knee and took her hand in his. "Alexa, will you marry me?"

"You know," she said, happy tears forming in her eyes, "if you don't stop that, you're going to ruin the knees in those pants, and I don't plan to have any time at all for shopping or mending."

He stood, drawing her into his embrace. "Is that a yes?"

"You'd better believe it, cowboy," she said, and leaned into a kiss designed to create a whole new scale.

Notes and Acknowledgments

I am deeply indebted to Noël Bennett, whose work *The Weaver's Pathway: A Clarification of the "Spirit Trail" in Navajo Weaving* (Flagstaff, Arizona: Northland Press, 1974) inspired the theme of this book. Many of the Navajo words and ideas about "the weaving sickness," its cures, and the weaver's path, were collected from interviews she did with Navajo weavers.

The Navajo Weaving Tradition: 1650 to the Present, by Alice Kaufman and Christopher Selser (New York: E. P. Dutton, Inc., 1985), provided background on the history of Navajo weaving, regional designs and vegetal dyes, as well as exquisite full-color photographs of some of the loveliest examples (my favorites are the storm pattern rugs and the Two Gray Hills tapestry rugs in all-natural colors).

Details on the Hopi bridal trousseau came from

Frederick J. Dockstader's *Weaving Arts of the North American Indian* (revised), (New York: HarperCollins, Inc., 1983).

I was deliberately vague on the location of Grand Falls, but it exists—seasonally, that is—and is a spectacular natural wonder. The red sandstone wall with its pioneer names also exists, exactly where I said it is. Though I didn't know Virgil and Bertha Howard in 1958 when they added their names to the wall, they became close family friends during the years I lived near the fictional community of Rainbow Rock. Reuben Josiah Perkins, Sr., to whom the quote from Psalm 107:8 is attributed, is my great-grandfather.